DECADENT
Desire

ZURI DAY

⊕ HARLEQUIN® KIMANI™ ROMANCE

Recycling programs
for this product may
not exist in your area.

ISBN-13: 978-0-373-86523-9

Decadent Desire

HARLEQUIN®
™ www.Harlequin.com

Printed in U.S.A.

Zuri Day is the national bestselling author of almost two dozen novels, including the popular Drakes of California series. Her books have earned her a coveted *Publishers Weekly* starred review and a Top Ten Pick out of all the romances featured in *PW* Spring 2014. Day is a winner of EMMA and AALAS (African American Literary Awards Show) Best Romance Awards, among others, and a multiple *RT Book Reviews* Best Multicultural Fiction finalist. Drakes of California book six, *Crystal Caress*, was voted Book of the Year and garnered her yet another EMMA Award in 2016. Her work has been featured in several national publications including *RT Book Reviews*, *Publishers Weekly*, *Sheen*, *Juicy* and *USA TODAY*. She loves interacting with her fans, the DayDreamers, and when she sees them in person gives out free hugs! Contact her and find out more at zuriday.com.

Books by Zuri Day

Harlequin Kimani Romance

Visit the Author Profile page
at Harlequin.com for more titles.

For Gabriel Ken Robinson, my real-life hero.

Acknowledgments

I am blessed to work with Glenda Howard, who has made bringing the Drakes of California to life a total joy. Love you! The ever-supportive, classy Shannon Criss. You rock! Keyla Hernandez, amid a slew of story lines and schedules, you help keep me organized. Thanks bunches! The devil is in the details and copy editors edit the hell out of a manuscript. LOL. Thanks for being great at what you do. To the Kimani family, especially Nicki Night, Sheryl Lister, Wayne Jordan, A.C. Arthur, Deborah Mello, Cheris Hodges, Patricia Sargeant, Sherelle Green and Martha Kennerson. Y'all make my heart happy. Write on! To the romance queens, the BJs: Brenda Jackson and Beverly Jenkins. Thank you…for everything. To the DayDreamers, my wonderful readers, who have grown to love the Drake family as much as I do. I'll love you forever and appreciate your support. Remember…don't quit your daydream!

Chapter 1

Anyone passing by Walter and Claire Drake's vast farm property in the Louisiana countryside just east of New Orleans would have thought a public festival was in full swing. Or maybe that a mini carnival had been set up for the Fourth of July holiday. A few excited would-be patrons had, in fact, been turned away from the private event by security manning the gated entrance.

Only those related to or invited by a Drake family member could attend the family's twenty-fifth biennial reunion, where descendants of former slaves and the owners who held them came together to honor their shared heritage and the enduring legacy of friendship between the slave Nicodemus Drake and his owner, Pierre. The story that forever bonded them had been passed down for generations.

The two men had grown up together, more like brothers than anything else. While making the journey to relocate from New Orleans to California, Pierre had fallen ill. Nicodemus's knowledge of herbal remedies and holistic healing had saved his life. Pierre was forever indebted to Nicodemus. In his will, Pierre deeded over to his lifelong friend more than a hundred acres of pristine land in tony Temecula, California—Southern California's wine country. He'd also stipulated that upon his death, Nicodemus and his immediate family would be given their freedom. This indeed occurred, and while the families dispersed across the United States—including Nicodemus's son who settled in Northern California—the ties that bound them, black and white alike, remained strong. In 1967, amid social unrest and war protests, Walter's grandparents had joined with Pierre's side of the family and held the first Drake reunion. Fifty years later, they still reunited every two years—bigger and stronger than ever.

Julian Drake, the youngest son of the fourth-generation Northern California clan, sat among a group of his relatives in the large, cool tent that was centered among colorful bounce houses, carnival rides and games. They were being entertained by a group of brothers and cousins going up against wives and girlfriends in a friendly yet competitive game of *Family Feud*. As often was the case, Julian sat quiet, contemplative, taking in everything going on around him. He'd been this way since childhood—his brothers loud and boisterous, Julian observant. Saying nothing, and missing nothing, either. So much so that during a visit to Louisiana his mother, Jennifer, had voiced her concern to his grandmother Claire.

"Almost eighteen months and still not talking," Jennifer had whispered, afraid to say the words out loud.

Claire had given Jennifer's hand a reassuring pat. "Don't worry none about that child. He's a special one. Not in that way," she'd quickly added when Jennifer's eyes grew wide. "Not that we would love him any less if that's the case. But I mean special as in gifted, maybe even like Nicodemus, as I am told, able to see into the future. Don't worry. He'll talk when he's ready, and when he does, he'll have something meaningful to say."

Claire had been right. Two months later Julian uttered his first words, a complete sentence, to his next-oldest brother, Terrell. Julian had been reading a book. Terrell wanted to play a game. Julian had looked up and pointedly demanded, "Leave me alone."

Jennifer had breathed a sigh of relief. His interactions with siblings and friends gradually increased. But to this day, he was still mostly a man of few words. Although when spoken, his statements usually had value.

Terrell was the exact opposite. He was a talkative extrovert who commanded attention everywhere he went and was the perfect host for these rounds of family fun.

"Next question," Terrell said, holding up a card while standing between his cousin Diamond and her husband, Jackson, whose hands were poised below bright red cowbells that served as buzzers.

"Name a side—"

Jackson clanged his bell. "Patricia!"

Men groaned. Women laughed. Julian smiled.

Terrell placed a hand on Jackson's shoulder. "The question is about a side dish, dude, not a side piece."

Jackson feigned shock. "What kind of man do you think I am? I thought you were going to say side*kick*." He winked at Julian.

"Who's Patricia?" Diamond crossed her arms in mock anger.

"Who cares?" Faye, the wife of Julian's cousin Dexter, asked. "Finish the question so Diamond can answer and we can win the game!"

Julian studied Faye's serious expression. She looked as if she were preparing to treat a patient rather than watch the ladies take a round of *Family Feud*. He hadn't gotten the chance to know her well but felt a shared camaraderie with the doctor, even though her title was MD instead of PsyD. In their last conversation, he'd discovered her heart for the less fortunate and had promised that once his internship ended and he started up his private practice, he'd offer monthly free counseling sessions at her clinic in San Diego. Since then he'd talked with his mother and decided to do the same on a more regular basis at the community center his family had built in their hometown. Every member of the family contributed in some way, including Terrell's twin sister, Teresa, who along with Faye and two women from Pierre's side of the family were now laughing and high-fiving at the women having beaten the men.

All of the couples were well matched, he reasoned, observing their effortless interactions. Even those with opposite personalities, like Faye and Dexter, who was as easygoing and extroverted as she was serious and subdued. Their dynamics reminded him of his own relationship. Nicki Long, his on-again, off-again girlfriend since college, was a private but sociable butterfly and professional dancer who fluttered seamlessly and graciously throughout life both on and off the stage. Watching the other couples made him miss her even more than he had since moving back to Paradise Cove three months ago.

Dexter walked by Julian and bopped him on the head. "Thanks a lot, genius!"

A nickname, but also the truth. Julian's IQ was near genius level—part of the being special his grandmother Claire had alluded to when he was a babe.

"For what? I wasn't even playing."

"That's his point," Terrell deadpanned, taking a seat beside Julian. "We needed that sharp mind of yours to best those conniving women. Now we're going to have to endure their endless ribbing for the next two years. All because of you!"

"No, because of Jackson and his sidekicks."

"Don't put all the blame on me." Jackson was more than ready to defend himself. He looked pointedly at Terrell. "I'm not the one who named sparrow as a bird that people eat."

"Hey." Terrell shrugged. "Chicken, turkey and duck had already been mentioned. Those are the only ones I…" His voice trailed off as he looked beyond Julian. "Is that who I think it is?"

Jackson looked up. "Who do you think it is?"

"Julian, isn't that your girl?"

Julian turned his head in the direction Terrell and Jackson were focused.

Nicki? He slowly rose from the chair as a tall, fit woman wearing a bright yellow maxi and a devilish smile walked toward him. She was with his youngest sister, London, who, given the look on her face, had obviously been in on the surprise.

He held out his arms to wrap her in a hug. "What are you doing here?"

"Milo decided to let us enjoy the holiday after all."

"The same director who works y'all for twelve hours a day, the one you questioned had a heart?"

"Yep. Guess there's something beating in there besides a drum after all. I texted London to surprise you and caught the first plane out."

"Surprised?" London asked, her smile widening.

"Delighted." His eyes drank in Nicki like a parched man guzzling water. "Let me take you around to meet everybody. Are you hungry? Can I get you a drink?"

Nicki laughed. "Okay, yes and yes."

"Hey, Nicki!"

"Hello, Terrell." She accepted his hug.

"You remember Atka, Teresa's husband."

"Of course. My mom still raves about your company's salmon that I had shipped to her house."

"And my cousin Jackson."

Nicki waved. "Hello."

Both were actually in-laws, but the Drakes disregarded that fact. Family was family. After going around to those nearby, Julian reached for Nicki's hand and headed toward the food tent. "We'll say hi to my parents and then get something to eat. You look beautiful, by the way."

"Thank you."

"You feel good, too. In fact—" he pulled her closer "—why don't we make our plates to go and find a more private place to…enjoy the meal?"

"Are we still talking about food?" she teased.

"Definitely not."

"Ha!"

Exactly thirty-nine minutes later, Julian and Nicki had successfully and surreptitiously left the farm, driven to a four-star hotel and checked in. Here, within the confines of a single room with a king bed, the quiet, studious doctor showed the wilder, passionate side that few would imagine. The door had barely closed when he reached for the hem of Nicki's maxi and backed her up to the bed.

"Julian, wait!"

"Shh. No talking."

They collapsed on the bed. Julian planted several kisses across Nicki's face before plunging his tongue into her mouth, his hungry, scalding kiss outmatched only by an ever-hardening shaft grinding against her thigh for proof of his ardent desire. He broke the kiss and tugged at her dress. She lifted her hips enough to free the unwanted material from beneath her body, then pulled the dress up and over her head and tossed it to the floor. His shirt quickly followed. Then pants, bra and undies. Julian groaned and delivered another hot kiss before his mouth left hers and went on a journey along the skin he'd missed immensely since Nicki's last visit to Paradise Cove over a month ago. He nibbled the sensitive area by her collarbone before inching down to modest breasts, pulling a hardened nipple into his mouth even as his hand traveled lower to Nicki's shaved treasure. He slid a finger along lips already creamy and teased her pearl with his fingertip even as his tongue caressed her other nipple.

"Ah!"

Her cry of pleasure made him smile as he continued to cherish every inch of her body with the same focus and attention to detail that he applied in professional life. Positioning himself between her legs, he scooted farther down, planted kisses on her pelvis, down her inner thighs, his tongue on a languid journey down the length of a leg solid and defined from years of lessons in tap, modern and jazz. She pulled her legs up and away from him, parted them in a perfect inverted split in the air. Her exposed, rock-hard pearl sent a clear message of what she wanted next.

He got the memo and without hesitation drew the nub into his mouth and then plunged his tongue inside her. Swirling, tickling, licking her joy trail as though it were chocolate ice cream. She ground herself against him. Short bursts of breath hinting of her impending climax. Just as she erupted, he replaced his tongue with several inches of hard passion and continued loving her.

Julian wasn't a dancer, but one couldn't tell. A disciplined workout regimen and martial arts training kept his six-foot-one-inch frame in shape, ready for several rounds of lovemaking. Finally, after Nicki's third orgasm, he gave in to his own shuddering release. A thin sheen of perspiration covered them both as he folded back the flowered spread, pulled away the cool white top sheet and covered them.

"See how much I missed you?" he asked, using his finger to smooth strands of dampened hair behind Nicki's ear.

"I felt how much." Her face was turned away from him, but Julian heard the smile in her voice.

"You sure I can't talk you into leaving New York, moving to the West Coast and ending this notion of a long-distance relationship? I can't see not having you, not having this—" he caressed her booty "—on a regular basis. Can you?"

Nicki turned to face him. "I almost died this month without having you around to do what you do, and very well, I might add. Of course I want to be with you. But you know I can't. I'm not the lead in this show, but it is Broadway. When are you coming to see the show?"

"I don't know, but I'd love to be there opening night. When does it start?"

"Next month."

"August? Isn't that unusual?"

"It's rare. Most shows open during the fall. We're hoping that being one of the few new shows next month will translate into a strong box office showing. What about you? Ready to open for business?"

"I already have a few clients. The office will open in two to three weeks, depending on how quickly I can hire an assistant. Mom worked with an interior designer friend to create the type of environment I want—professional and relaxing at the same time. It'll be finished by the time I get back in town."

"From here?"

"No, from Chicago. I fly there for a conference that begins on Wednesday."

"Office up and running, clients on the schedule. Sounds like the transition from intern to private practice was easy."

"There were challenges."

"Obviously none you couldn't handle."

He smiled, swiped the tip of her nose. "What's your point?"

"The point is that you can make opening night, maybe even bring some of your family along. It's going to be a great show. The Rapunzel fairy tale has been done before, but never like this."

"With Rapunzel rapping her lines? I think not. Bet those DJs in the '70s talking over beats had no idea what a revolution in music they were creating, a style that would end up on Broadway and take over the music world."

"The genre has definitely outlasted its critics. The show involves hip-hop, jazz, even country. It will appeal to a wide audience, which is why I think the chances of *A Hair's Tale* succeeding on Broadway are very good. It's a limited run right now. Only sixteen weeks. But if it remains as popular as it is now, the show can get extended indefinitely. Have an unbelievable run, like *The Lion King*, *Phantom* and *Cats*. As long as it's on Broadway, I want to be playing my role!"

"You're dramatic." A caress suggested it was a part of her that he enjoyed. "I'll tell them about it, see if they want to join me."

Nicki turned, her gaze loving as she took a finger and outlined Julian's thick brows, his aquiline nose and Cupid's bow lips. "Thank you, Doctor," she whispered.

"You're welcome, my private dancer," he cooed, brushing his hand across her long, silky tresses before pulling her into his arms, kissing her deeply and silently vowing to find a way to permanently shorten the distance between them.

Chapter 2

Julian Drake, PsyD. A bit pretentious, Julian thought as he stopped and observed the gold-and-platinum name plaque on the door of his practice. His mother had purchased and mounted it as a welcome-home surprise, along with the office suite they'd given him for earning his psychology doctorate earlier than most and breezing through an eighteen-month internship with ease.

He appreciated the gesture, even though the nameplate wasn't his style at all. A plain black plastic slider with white lettering would have been fine with him, and the office suite had a few more rooms than he needed. Especially now while just getting started. His parents, Ike and Jennifer, were understandably proud, and ecstatic that he'd decided to open his practice in Paradise Cove instead of on the East Coast as Nicki had wanted. That she hadn't joined him was a disappointment for his family and devastating for him. His family loved Nicki. Her tomboyish ways with his brothers helped her fit right in, and her knack for style with a bohemian edge, along with being a professional dancer, made for a lot in common with his sisters. Jennifer had even approached Nicki with the idea of periodic dance workshops at the Drake Community Center. As much as he'd wanted it, Julian knew the chances of Nicki relocating with him was a long shot. After she got a major role in a Broadway show, he knew there was no shot at all. The entertainment world was all abuzz about the talented young writer who'd created the show and the composer who'd scored the work. His sister had even heard about it. When Julian told London about Nicki's invitation, she'd excitedly asked to join him, but the preview shows were sold out.

Julian was eager to get his practice up and running. The busier he was, the less time he'd have to think about how much he missed Nicki.

His cell phone vibrated. Had he thought her up? Retrieving it from his jacket pocket, he unlocked the door while answering the call.

"Dr. Drake." He hit the speaker button and continued through the reception area to the spacious corner office he occupied.

"Yes, Doctor. This is Natalie Moore from Superior Staffing. You left a message with our service last night requesting a call."

Julian immediately recognized the voice. "Natalie as in the Nat Pack?"

A short pause and then, "Do I know you?"

"Yes, you do. It's Julian."

"The Julian Drake I picked on all through grade school?"

"I think it lasted through junior high, and yes, it's me."

"No way! And you're a doctor now? Not surprising, since you left all your classmates behind in the dust. You skipped, what, one or two years?"

"More like doubled up on some and tested out of others. They didn't really skip me."

"However it happened, you graduated at sixteen. You'd already been gone a couple months when I found out. I can't believe you remember me."

"Didn't at first. Your married name threw me. But I'll never forget that high-pitched voice."

"And I'll never forget you had no voice at all. Always so quiet. And I'm divorced, by the way. Would have reverted to Johnson, but I have a son. The boy genius Julian, a doctor. That fits you. Will you be working at the urgent-care center that just opened up?"

"I'm a psychologist, not a medical doctor. I'm opening a private practice."

Another pause, this one a bit longer. "Come to give my dad some competition, huh? He's the go-to shrink in this town. Has treated patients here for over thirty years. So good luck with that."

"I have no desire to compete with Dr. Johnson or anyone else. Mental illnesses and behavioral disorders have steadily increased through the years that he's practiced and are still on the rise, which means, unfortunately, there are likely to be enough clients for both of us."

"That's what a couple other doctors thought. One still has an office here, though I heard she teaches at a community college to supplement her income. Guess the one or two people who slipped past my father weren't enough for her to pay the bills."

"Thanks for the encouragement."

"You're welcome."

Julian pondered Natalie's words as he gazed out the window. It was a beautiful day. During the festivities in Louisiana, the mercury had climbed to ninety degrees and above. Too hot for Julian, even for July. Or any other month. He much preferred the seventies experienced during Northern California summers. The office's location on the building's fifteenth floor offered unobstructed views of the town's tony square and the sprawling fields and ranches of Paradise Valley beyond it. His brother Warren owned one of those ranches. He thought how good a horse ride would feel but knew that with the work ahead of him, today wouldn't be when he got to do it.

"Where'd you graduate and do your internship?"

"Graduated from Columbia." Julian walked back to his desk and sat. "Interned in New York."

"Impressive, Doctor. Why'd you decide to come back here?"

Julian looked at his watch. Time to focus on the matter at hand—hiring an assistant. If she was as nosy now as she had been in high school, the Natalie he remembered could keep him on the phone all afternoon.

"Probably the same reason you did, to do business in my hometown. Speaking of which, I assume your call is regarding the information I filled out online?"

"Yes, Superior Staffing is my company, and yes, PC is still a very small town."

They shared a laugh. "Indeed. Will you be able to assist me, considering I'm viewed as your dad's competition?"

"Ha! Dad has probably forgotten more than you'll learn."

"Ouch!"

"Just calling it like I see it. You're no competition for him. As for an assistant, I do have a couple qualified recruits in mind who, based on what I know so far, would be good matches. At least from the online questionnaire that you filled out."

"So how do we proceed? I'd like to get someone hired as quickly as possible."

"Normally I'd set up the first appointment and send them over at your earliest convenience. But since it's you, a friend I've known since grade school, I think a follow-up interview is in order, one done in person so I can be sure to select the most appropriate candidates for the position. What about dinner tomorrow night at Acquired Taste?"

"I'm busy most evenings. How about lunch, around noon?"

"Perfect. See you then."

"And Natalie, no practical jokes, okay? The little kid is all grown up."

"You sure have, and quite nicely. I pulled up your profile online."

"Good. Then I'll be easy to recognize. See you tomorrow."

Julian dodged Natalie's flirty comment. He remembered her popularity in high school and had known several of the guys she'd dated. Pretty girl. Funny, too. He wanted her assistance in finding a competent assistant, but nothing more.

"Another great show, Nicki!"

"Thanks, hon." Nicki hugged Paige, her friend and cast mate. "Had to take it to the next level to shine beside you!"

"That's right, girl! Razzle!"

"Dazzle!" They high-fived. "If these previews are any indication, opening night is going to be huge."

"Is Julian coming?"

"That's the plan. What about Mike?"

"I don't know. He's always working."

"Hmm, the detective sounds like someone else I know."

The two laughed, locking arms as they walked down the dark and narrow backstage hallway to the exit just off Forty-Ninth Street. As usual, a group of theatergoers circled the exit, waiting for a chance to get a snapshot. Maybe even an autograph or a selfie. Most were there for Paige, the famous pop celebrity playing Rapunzel. But a lot of fans loved the best friend added in the modern retelling of the classic fairy tale and waited for Nicki, who played her. Though tired, Nicki obliged them. Countless times, she'd been that fan, waiting for her favorite star. Dying for an autograph. She'd dreamed of being that star since she was ten. And here she was.

Paige turned to her. "Hey, my car's here. Want a ride?"

"Seriously? Of course!"

The driver stood next to the rear car door he'd just

opened. "Good evening, ladies." A nod and smile accompanied the formal greeting.

"Joe, this is Nicki. Nicki, Joe."

"Hello, Joe."

They slid into the back seat of a roomy town car. Nicki rubbed her hand across the soft leather seat. "Is this one of the perks of being the star?"

"Thanks to my agent. I wouldn't have thought to request it on my own."

Nicki settled against the seat and sighed. "Lifestyles of the rich and famous."

Paige leaned forward toward a panel of buttons and raised the privacy partition.

"Ooh, fancy! Just like in the movies."

"I thought you'd like it. But I put it up because you had something to tell me."

The reminder sat Nicki straight up. "Oh my gosh, girl, you won't believe it. And I'm telling you right now. This can't be repeated. If I hear it back, I'll know where to come."

"Don't you know you can trust me by now?"

Nicki did. The entertainment business was cutthroat. Jobs on Broadway were limited. Competition was fierce and few made friends, Nicki included. Paige had been the exception. The two had met while doing regional theater, ironically both having boy troubles at the time. They commiserated and eventually met each other's boyfriends—Julian and Mike. Shortly after the play ended, Paige moved to New York. They'd been besties ever since.

"Remember a couple years ago when Julian and I broke up?"

"Like the for-real breakup, because you turned down his marriage proposal and broke the guy's heart? Yep, I remember."

"Dang, Paige, did you have to say it like that?"

"To clarify which off-and-on we were talking about? Yes, I did. Besides, isn't that what happened?"

"Anyway…remember my rebound guy, the pro basketball player?" Nicki placed air quotes around his title.

"Told you that he played pro ball, left out that he hadn't had a contract in years?"

"I still can't believe I didn't google his ass."

Nicki paused and looked out the window. A mental replay of meeting Vince Edwards played in her mind.

Late-night party uptown. Private. Rooftop. Being beautiful seemed the price of admission. A stranger approached while she sipped a drink. Introduced himself as Vince Edwards, a pro basketball player. He'd sure looked the part. Tall, attractive. Muscles and dimples in all the right places, with enough raw manly swagger to bottle and sell. When they hugged she got goose bumps, but along with the excitement came a foreboding feeling. She ignored it and gave him her number.

A couple of weeks into the romantic whirlwind, behaviors began to surface that had reminded Nicki of her earlier apprehensiveness. The first was declaring his love for her a week after they met. The second was falling in love with her brownstone that—number three—he wanted to move into after the second week. Nicki saw more red flags after this request than those waved in Arrowhead Stadium at a Chiefs football game. But she'd continued to date him. Until the fourth reason—a woman named Brittany. The woman with whom he currently lived. The woman who'd threatened to kick him out for cheating, and not just with Nicki. In a calm, almost pleasant voice, the astute stranger had passed along a few pertinent details Vince had not shared. Multiple children. Gambling habit. No new sports contract or endorsement deals. Nicki thanked the woman and meant it. Got back with Julian a short time later, thankful she'd dodged a bullet.

"I thought you blocked his number."

"I did. A call came up private. I answered it without a second thought."

"What did he want?"

"Nothing much. Just wondered if I had twenty thousand dollars to loan him."

Paige screeched. "WTF?"

"Oh, and he needs it by Friday. Can you believe it?"

"How'd he figure you had that kind of money?"

"I guess because I'm on a Broadway stage."

"Even so, why'd he think you'd loan it to him?"

"That's where it really gets crazy. He's taking credit for the show I did in Atlanta shortly after we broke up. Says he pulled the strings that got me the job."

"Ooh, right! And he showed up backstage claiming y'all were a couple. Wasn't the director his sister or something?"

"Cousin, and it turned out only a distant one at that. He had nothing to do with me getting that job. I auditioned like everyone else. What a liar."

"You guys didn't even date that long. What was it, a month?"

"Barely."

"Jeez. So what did you say when he asked you?"

"What do you think I said? No! Then he had the nerve to ask me out!"

"What was your answer?" Paige asked, laughing.

"Hell no!"

Nicki tried not to laugh but was soon cracking up. Paige always made her feel better.

"Do you think he'll call again?"

"With the size of his ego? I don't doubt it."

They reached Paige's apartment building in trendy

SoHo. The driver dropped Paige off, headed toward the Brooklyn Bridge and twenty minutes later was at Nicki's place, a three-story brownstone that had been converted into two apartments. Hers was the larger one and occupied the two upper floors. It was spacious and airy, with tall ceilings and big windows to let in lots of natural light. Her respite from the grind of the theater district, where she practically lived six days a week.

"Bye, Joe." She blew a kiss to the driver, then opened the gate and hurried up the steps to the second-floor entrance. Within seconds she'd kicked off her shoes and walked to the kitchen in search of something sparkling with a kick. She wasn't much of a drinker, but a wine spritzer after two shows helped her wind down.

"Nothing," she mumbled, looking in the fridge. "Great."

Bypassing the heels she'd just kicked off, Nicki grabbed a pair of sandals from the hallway shoe rack and headed to the corner store that, luckily for her, stayed open until eleven. After picking out her favorite chardonnay and a liter of sparkling water, she headed back home. The street was sparsely populated and quiet, typical for this time on a Wednesday night. As she neared her walk-up, two men got out of a car parked in front. Ever the New Yorker, she was on instant alert but didn't pick up any negative vibes. They talked casually, even laughed as the driver tapped the key fob to lock the car. Nicki relaxed, stepped to the right to walk by them. The driver, to his left. She looked up, expecting a come-on. The man was not laughing. At all.

She took a step in the other direction. The passenger had come from the other side of the car and stood in front of her.

A frustrated sigh gave her the chance to quickly scan the areas behind and beside her. Suddenly the streets were empty. Not another person in sight. *Why didn't I buy groceries on Monday, instead of spending the day on Long*

Island catching up with friends? Instead of fifteen dollars and some change, her desire for a sparkling libation could cost a lot more. Her brownstone was only two doors down. If she could just get around them…

Summoning her Brooklyn-born-and-bred attitude, she raised to her full height of five foot eight and looked the man standing in front of her directly in the eye. At the same time, she positioned her house key between her index and middle fingers, ready to puncture a cheek or gouge out an eye.

"Let me by."

"Nicki Long, right?"

Caught entirely off guard, she couldn't hide her surprise. "Who are you?"

"Friends of Vince. Come to get the money you owe him."

Seriously? Vince's ego was bigger than she realized. But if he thought this Brooklyn babe could be intimated, he had another thought coming.

"You have the wrong Nicki. I don't owe Vince a thing." She took a step to go around the guy talking, the one on the right. He stepped, too, in front of her.

"Move," she commanded, now truly more annoyed than angry. "Vince has obviously lied to you, just like he did to me. I hope the promise of money wasn't one of them."

The tall, lanky driver studied his nails, wearing dark shades at almost midnight. "Vince did promise us money, as a matter of fact. From the money you owe him. So now instead of one problem—" he looked at his partner "—you have three."

"Look, I don't owe Vince. And I don't even know you, let alone owe you. You've got the wrong woman." Nicki pushed past him. A steely hand clamped onto her arm. Stopped her in her tracks. She whirled around.

"Let go of me." The driver increased the pressure. It hurt like heck. Her heart thudded erratically. But Nicki forced her features to remain relaxed. She pointedly looked at his hand on her arm and then into his eyes. "I said let. Me. Go."

"Hey, neighbor!"

Nicki's body almost sagged in relief. Miss Frances was an elaborative gossip and a constant snoop, but at this very moment Nicki could have kissed her on the mouth.

"Good evening!" She pushed past the men and walked toward the gate where Miss Frances stood wearing a flowered robe and a sleeping cap over pink foam rollers, her squinted eyes trained on the men now walking toward the car.

"We'll be at the show," the driver said, fake friendly. "Rapunzel," he added, making sure she knew he knew which one.

"We'll be sure to look for you." Nicki turned and watched the passenger taunt her as he opened his car door. "Break a leg."

A shiver ran down Nicki's spine. She turned away. Miss Frances continued to stare at the car as it started up and eased away from the curb.

"QZZ, zero, zero, zero, four."

"Ma'am?"

"The license plate number. Hurry up and write it down."

Nicki repeated the number, impressed that her neighbor had thought to get it. "I'll remember it. Thank you so much, Miss Frances. I don't know what would have happened if you hadn't come out when you did."

"I saw you trying to get past them. When the second one came over and blocked the walk, I figured it was trouble." Miss Frances turned keen eyes on Nicki. "You don't know those men?"

Nicki shook her head. "No."

"They obviously know you, came right to your doorstep. What did they want?"

"They had me confused with somebody else."

"How could that be when they're coming to your show?" Miss Frances's gaze was unflinching. Clearly she was unconvinced.

Nicki was equally convinced that what the two men wanted from her was not only something she wouldn't give, but also something her nosy, overly talkative neighbor didn't need to know.

"Thanks again for coming out to check on me. You more than likely prevented a crime."

"Watching out for each other is what neighbors do."

Nicki gave Miss Frances a quick hug and headed toward her gate.

"Watch yourself," Miss Frances yelled behind her. "Remember, those men said they'd see you tomorrow."

Nicki gave a final wave as she hurried up the steps and into her apartment. There was no need for Miss Frances's reminder. What the men had said—and even more so how they'd said it—was something that Nicki knew she'd never forget.

Once inside she opened the wine, poured a liberal amount into a goblet and took a long drink. She added some sparkling water and climbed the stairs to her bedroom. With each step her heart slowed and her hands shook less. The past several minutes replayed like a video in her mind. Even as it happened, it had felt like a movie. As if it were someone else. After recording the license number on a pad by her bed, she dialed Vince's number. It went to voice mail.

"If what happened tonight happens again, I'm going to the police. I will not be harassed, and I certainly will not be threatened by the likes of you or those fools you sent over tonight. Their actions were recorded. So is this phone call. Leave me alone, Vince Edwards. Goodbye."

She hung up, exhausted. Massaged her tense neck and shoulders. Despite the bravado in her message to Vince, the sinister-looking bullies had left Nicki shaken. She wondered if by chance the store's surveillance camera had picked up those guys accosting her tonight. She made a mental note to check with the owner tomorrow. For now, she wanted to go to sleep and escape a nightmare named Vince.

Chapter 3

She'd planned to tell no one what happened last night. Especially Paige, because Nicki knew she would worry. But a few days later, while Nicki waited with Paige for the pop star's car to arrive, the words tumbled out.

"If my neighbor hadn't come out when she did," she finished, "I don't know what might have happened. A part of me wants to believe this was just a scare tactic to see if I could be frightened into sending the cash."

Paige's look was doubtful. "And the other part?"

"Really wishes those store cameras could have captured their images so that I'd have concrete evidence of how they harassed me."

"But their car was on the tape?" Nicki nodded. "Then take that along with a statement from your neighbor and file a police report. You can't ignore this, Nicki, or wish it away. I hope that night was the end of it, but if not, you'll want to have everything that happened documented. Do you still have the messages Vince left on your phone?"

"I think so."

"You need to keep all of that, and if he ever calls again, record it. And you need to tell Julian."

"Why would I do that?"

"Because the more people who are aware of what's happening, the better any future case might be. And because he's the man who loves you."

Joe waved as he pulled the car to the curb.

Nicki waved back and turned to walk away.

Paige called after her, "Where are you going? Joe will take you home."

"And get used to such lavish star treatment? I'm fine on the subway."

Paige waved off the comment and walked toward her. "Marry Julian and you'll have your own driver." She lowered her voice. "I know your real reason for preferring the train. To get off the subject of telling Julian what's going on. This business with Vince is out of control. He needs to know about it."

"I'll think about it." Nicki started walking again. Tossed a parting line over her shoulder. "See you mañana."

She headed to the downtown trains, jumping on the Brooklyn-bound number three. Passing a couple empty seats as the car swayed and wove its way through the underground tunnels, she placed a shoulder against a pole with the practiced ease of a native New Yorker, checking emails and reading texts. One was from Julian. He'd wished her *merde*, a dancer's good luck, as he did most nights. Made her think of Paige and the proposal that had happened months before Julian began his internship.

It had been lovely. Lit up on the marquee in the heart of Times Square. He'd gone to one knee, pulled out a telltale blue box and everything. A crowd had gathered, oohed and ahhed. He'd looked so hopeful. But she couldn't say yes. She'd smiled and hugged him excitedly, making the crowd think she accepted so he wouldn't be embarrassed. But later on she broke the truth. New York was her soul, Broadway her goal. That's when he decided they needed a break.

And then Vince happened. She'd heard there'd been no shortage of women vying to claim the spot as Julian's girlfriend that she'd vacated. A couple of them she knew. Word was he hadn't dated, had focused on work. Once they got back together, she found out why and felt even worse about her rebound fling. Her rejection had hurt him as deeply as he loved her, a love so strong that when she reached out to him several months later, he took her back, no problem.

The train reached her stop. It was late. Only one other person got off with her. She walked to the stairs and climbed up them, trying to ignore the fearful thought that the duo she'd started calling Bert and Ernie might be waiting for her. Time for a diversion. It was either that or a panic attack. Pulling out her phone, she called Julian. Contrary to Paige's advice, she would not tell him about what was going on. Julian didn't know about that ill-fated tryst. She intended to keep it that way.

"Hey, babe. Thanks for the encouraging text. Didn't read it until after, but the show was—" Nicki drew in a sharp breath as she watched a dark-colored sedan race toward her. Instinct took over. She ran against the light, chancing a look back as she crossed the street. Caught the first two letters on the license plate as the car zoomed through the intersection and continued on its way. Not after her. Just in a hurry. She remembered the license number Miss Frances had given her. The one she'd just seen wasn't it.

She eased out of the storefront entryway, feeling silly. Paranoid much? She felt someone's gaze and looked up to see an old man watching her intently. Could only imagine how she must have looked, running when no one was chasing her. Hiding from someone that he couldn't see. She looked down and realized the call to Julian was still live. God, no. Had she made a sound? Nicki quickly pushed the end button, praying that somehow in the frenzy a message that would sound weird at best, maybe even frightening, wouldn't go through. Minutes later a text came through. Her prayer had not been answered.

Babe, what's going on? Where are you?

She continued the short distance to her house, formulating an answer on the way. Just inside her home, she dropped her bag and texted back.

Sorry about that. Just wanted to beat the light, that's all.

Nicki continued up the stairs to her bedroom, hoping the casual answer would suffice. After several minutes had passed, she thought it had. She took a shower, washed her hair and slipped into a pair of comfy cotton pj's. Grabbing her phone, she continued downstairs for a cup of chamomile. Julian had called. Left a message and a text. Not only did he not buy her lie, he told her he'd see her on opening night, in person, to find out the truth. Damn, damn, damn!

One week after that text exchange and ten minutes before curtain, the Drake entourage entered the theater and were ushered to the third row in the orchestra's center section. They'd flown in for opening night on a company plane. A limo service met them at the private airstrip, with premium champagne and appetizers for the thirty-minute ride into the theater district. The men debonair, the women beautiful, they commanded the attention of the entire audience. Julian took the center seat. To his right was his oldest brother, Ike Jr., with his wife, Quinn. No question whose decision it was to accept his invitation. Ike, ten years older than his pretty wife, detested hip-hop or any similar sounding music. Or he had, until Quinn came into the picture. Of all Julian's brothers, Ike's temperament most closely matched his own. That the conservative executive who almost slept in a business suit tonight sported a matching shirt and slacks set from their fashion designer brother-in-law Ace Montgomery's collection was proof of how Quinn had relaxed him.

Julian loved observing the laid-back Ike, almost as much as the fact that California's next senator sat on his other side. After serving as mayor of Paradise Cove for several years, another brother, Niko, two years younger than Ike, was on a tireless campaign to represent the Golden State in the next election. He and attorney wife Monique crisscrossed the state tirelessly, so much so that the family staged a mock intervention to force a weekend of rest. The bribe? Tickets to Nicki's sold-out show. A Monday morning meeting with a political think tank had been thrown in also, but Julian chose not to focus on that. His brother was here, relaxed, laughing with Terrell, Julian's next oldest brother, in town with his wife, Aliyah. All in attendance to support his girl.

Their gesture was much appreciated. For almost a decade, his focus had been on getting his PsyD and completing his internship. Everything else had taken a back seat, including Nicki and his family. He blamed that fact on why Nicki turned down his marriage proposal. As for the people around him who shared his name? He hadn't realized how much he'd missed them until just now.

He nudged Ike. "Ready to get the party started?"

"What I'd start would more likely be a mass exit."

"Honey!" Quinn smacked his forearm. "That didn't sound very supportive."

"Hey, I'm here, aren't I?"

"Yes, with a pair of earplugs in your pocket."

Julian leaned forward toward Quinn. "You're kidding, right?" She shook her head. "Bro, really?"

"Guilty as charged."

Julian and Quinn shared a sigh of exasperation. She watched him idly tapping the chair arm with his fingers. "Nervous?"

"Excited."

"When's the last time you saw her perform?"

New Orleans, Julian thought with a smile, remembering their secret family reunion getaway. "It's been a while."

"London's going to hate that she missed it."

Niko's wife, Monique, sat next to Quinn. "All London is thinking about is fashion week. She and Ace are busy tightening up next week's show-stopping finale."

Julian's youngest sister, London, was a superstar model, her husband, Ace, a model turned fashion mogul.

"Fashion week is impressive," Quinn said, her eyes sparkling as she eyed the stage. "But this is Broadway."

As if on cue, the lights dimmed.

The stage went completely black. A single drumbeat burst out of the darkness. *Boom cha. Boom cha.* Then several more percussion instruments along with a sequencer delivering an old-school scratch over syncopated beats, building with every note. Lights, like stars, began to flicker everywhere. On stage and off.

A group of dancers appeared, Nicki among them, lithe, graceful, beautiful, twirling and gyrating and skipping across the stage. Julian watched. Focused. Entranced. Her body seemed a mass of barely contained energy mixed with soulful joy and childlike timidity, personifying the young character she portrayed. A bodysuit clung to her like a second skin, the crystals covering it catching the light, mixing with the twinkling orbs around her that made her a star as well. His heart swelled with pride and, but for strong discipline, another body part would have also grown in size. She was beautiful and talented, amazing and perfect. And she was his girl.

The dance ended. For a second no one moved, then as one, the theater erupted in a round of earsplitting applause mixed with whistles and yells. The second song in the act began, a solo by Rapunzel, and ninety minutes later the audience had to catch their breaths from the wild, exhilarating ride on which they'd been taken. Shortly after the show ended, an assistant came to escort the Drake family backstage.

Behind the door was a crush of sponsors, reporters, actors and their family members, all vying for space in the close, humid quarters. Julian spotted Nicki across the room. She posed with the actor who'd played Rapunzel. Camera flashes temporarily brightened their drab surroundings. A dozen conversations happened at once, a din that made talking at length impossible. He motioned for the others to follow him. Nicki saw his gesture. She whispered to Rapunzel, who looked their way and joined Nicki as she walked over.

Nicki hugged Julian before turning to Paige. "You remember Julian."

"Of course. Hey, handsome!"

"Hey, Paige. Excellent show." They shared a brief hug and air-kisses.

"And this is part of the Drake family."

"My pleasure to meet everybody." Paige smiled as she took in the beautiful tableau. "I've heard so much about all of you."

"All good, I hope," Niko said.

"No, she told me the truth."

Amid the laughter, Nicki introduced Paige to the rest of the family before leading the way through a narrow, dimly lit hallway to the door with a star that bore her name. Once inside, Julian allowed the others to offer their congrats before once again pulling Nicki into his arms. "You were amazing, baby."

"You liked it?"

"I loved it."

She pulled away to look at him. "Thanks for the flowers and the champagne. They're wonderful."

"So are you."

Niko stepped up to the couple. "I hate to break up this lovefest, but it's hot as heck in this shoe box. A star like you can't command a larger dressing room?"

"This is a larger one," Nicki deadpanned. "And I'm not a star yet, but thank you. Now get out of here. Give me a few minutes to change, and I'll meet you by the side exit. Except you," she finished, reaching for Julian's hand as the others exited. "You can help me undress."

"I haven't seen you in a month, girl," Julian whispered, running a hand down her back and cupping her butt. "Seeing all that loveliness and not getting a taste will be a pretty tall order."

She wrapped her arms around his neck. Gave him a peck on the lips. "It'll be worth the wait."

He kissed her back, deepened it with a swipe of his tongue to part her lips as he reached behind her and undid her zipper. Her last costume, a long, frilly number of sequins and lace, fell to the floor as Julian ran his hands along her torso, searching for and finding pert nipples ready to tweak. He lowered his mouth and pulled one in between his teeth, walked them toward the dressing table.

"Julian!"

"Just a little bit…"

He lifted her with the finesse of a dancing partner, set her on the table and positioned himself between her legs. The belt buckle was unfastened. Pants came unzipped. He reached for his ever-hardening shaft, rubbed the tip along her leg as he eased it toward her quivering folds and…

Knock! "Nicki? You in there?"

"Don't answer it," Julian whispered.

"It's not locked." Nicki shimmied off the table and reached for her robe. "Yeah, I'm in here." She cracked the door.

An assistant peeked her head in. "A reporter from *Variety* is here for you. A bunch of fans, too."

"Out in five minutes."

Shortly afterward, Nicki emerged from the dressing room looking fresh and effervescent, as though she'd emerged from a nap, not just performed a nonstop, high-energy show. Hair pulled into a topknot, face nearly devoid of makeup and eyes glowing, she wore a long, loose maxi with bold geometric prints, clunky jewelry and sandals. One could have easily mistaken her for a model instead of a dancer, and many had. Julian walked beside her, a strong but quiet presence amid the crowd.

"Nicki! Nicki!" Fans and the press clamored for her attention. She spent a moment with the reporters, then walked over to where dozens of fans held out programs and other memorabilia for her to sign. While she posed for a couple selfies, Julian texted Niko and requested the limo be brought around to the side entrance. When he turned back, she was rushing toward him.

"Let's go," she muttered, not stopping. "Where's the car?"

Julian quickly spotted Niko standing beside a white stretch limo and waving. He reached for her hand. "Come on."

He helped her into the limo. She fell back against the seat, clearly relieved.

"Looks like they didn't want to let you go back there," Niko teased.

"Yeah." Nicki glanced out the window, then turned to Julian. "Where are we eating? I'm starved."

"I've handled that," Terrell said. "Driver, we're ready."

The limo pulled away from the curb. Julian put an arm around Nicki. "What was that about?"

"What?"

"You left as though you were running away from someone."

Quinn overheard him. "What, someone freaked her out?"

All other conversation halted. Eyes turned toward her. "Julian is overexamining my hasty exit. I was simply ready to go."

He leaned over and spoke softly in her ear. "Ready to go, or trying to beat another light?"

She laughed off the remark, and in the familiar surroundings of New York City interacted more confidently with Julian's powerful family. She regaled them with stories of life in the city that never slept, including some memorable college moments with Julian before she'd dropped out to pursue dancing. Anyone looking on would see a beautiful, carefree woman out on the town. But Julian wasn't fooled. He was not only a doctor of behavioral study who'd graduated with honors, but a highly observant man who'd seen every side of Nicki. Something was going on with her. Something she obviously didn't want to share. They were in the city to celebrate her opening night, so he wouldn't push. But he wouldn't forget, either. It looked like he now had two problems—how to get Nicki to leave New York and move to California, and how to find out what was behind the urgency in his gut that made him want to hasten that move.

Chapter 4

"Are you sure it was him?"

Though she hadn't gotten much sleep due to the Drakes' late departure from New York City, Nicki was up before seven o'clock. It was either that or keep lying in bed thinking through a continuous replay of what happened last night. Instead, she'd been shimmying into a pair of running shorts when Paige called with the critics' glowing reviews. The conversation had quickly shifted to less optimistic news.

"Paige, I'm positive. It was Vince. I don't think he saw the show, but he was there waiting on the sidewalk by the stage door. I saw him as soon as we walked outside."

"Maybe he did see it and came back there to congratulate you."

"Then why didn't he? Why is it that he started toward me, but when he saw Julian he quickly turned around and went the other way? I swear I don't know what's up with that guy, but his stalker-like ways are starting to freak me out."

"Did he call you?"

"Nope. But I tried calling him. Went to voice mail again."

"Did you leave a message?"

"Same as last time. Said I didn't have money to lend him and to leave me alone or I'd call the police." Nicki rubbed away the goose bumps that had suddenly popped up on her arms. "I want to believe he'll do as I asked, but there was something about him when I saw him last night. A desperate kind of look in his eyes…"

"I think you should go to the police."

"And say what? That a guy asked me for a loan and then came to my show?"

"That's not how you told it to me."

"It's how the police will see it."

"What about the black sedan?"

"What about it? Other than the license plate number, I don't have anything to prove that story. Even that isn't concrete proof those guys threatened me or were even by my house. They could deny it and the police would deduce that I could have written that number down from anywhere." Nicki's phone beeped. "Oh my God, Paige. I think this is him. See you tonight."

"Be careful. Record the call!"

Nicki clicked over. "Hello?" She opened her settings, looking for a record button.

"Hey, Nicki."

"Vince. What's going on? Why are you stalking me?"

"Stalking you? What are you talking about?"

She scrolled through her settings, pushed the call icon. Scrolled. Where was the record feature and why hadn't she tried finding it before now?

"The other night at the show."

"Yeah, I was there. So were hundreds of other people."

"You saw the show?"

"Of course. Why else would I be there?"

"Um, let's see, I can think of about twenty thousand reasons, unless you found someone else to give you the loan."

"Oh, that. No, I haven't found anyone, and the guys I owe are stepping up the pressure."

"Like you did to me by sending over your thuggish friends?"

She heard an anguished sigh. "I didn't send them over, Nicki. Not how you're thinking, anyway. I told them you owed me money. I didn't tell them to go over and collect it."

"Then how'd they know where I live?" Silence. "Exactly." Nicki gave up trying to find the record button. It was too hard to search, think and talk at the same time. "What you're doing is not cool, Vince. And while I'm sorry you've gotten yourself into a predicament, there's nothing I can do to help you."

"Not even with some of it—say, five thousand, or ten?"

"Why do you think I have that kind of money to loan out, or that I'd give it to you even if I did?"

"Because at one time you cared about me."

That much was true, Nicki secretly admitted. She'd fallen hard and fast for the tall charmer. Theirs had been a brief romance, but it also had been a whirlwind of intense fun and loving. Before it wasn't.

"Because even though I was a dog in the time that we hung out, my feelings for you were real. I wish I'd understood what a gift it was to have you in my life, but it took you leaving for me to find that out."

"I don't know what you want me to say. I don't hate you, and I can't loan you money."

"Is that guy the reason you won't go out, the one with you at the show last night?"

"Look, Vince, I've got to go."

"Just tell me. Is that your boyfriend? If so, I'll leave you alone, for real this time."

"You promise you won't call again?"

"Not even as friends? I like you, okay?"

"You don't even know me."

"I know what I like."

"Yes. That was my boyfriend. He and I have been together a very long time."

"How long?"

"More than five years." Nicki realized her mistake at once.

"So I'm not the only cheater on the phone."

"I didn't cheat. We'd broken up when you and I got together, and you and I only dated a month. New York is full of good women. Find one of them and treat her the way you should have treated me and all of the women who've been hurt by your actions. Okay?"

"Okay. Bye, Nicki."

Nicki hung up the phone, exhausted, depleted. Getting through that conversation without losing it had probably taken years off her life. What was that about? Declarations of love and sincere-sounding compliments?

She walked into her closet, mumbling, "Probably running the same kind of game that got me with him in the first place."

Minutes later, earbuds firmly in place, Nicki pushed past the gate to her brownstone and hit the sidewalk running. She'd done way too little of it lately, none since what happened the other night. The conversation with Vince had been taxing, but in a way it had also freed her. He'd said he would leave her alone. She believed it.

Running in place, she looked around her. How she loved the borough called Brooklyn. Bright, bustling, colorful, diverse. Nicki knew Julian wanted her to move west. He hadn't mentioned it on this trip but that didn't matter. California was beautiful, true enough. But who would ever want to leave all this energy and feel like they were on vacation forever?

The light turned. Nicki jogged across the street, down the block and around the corner. She saw the bike, heard a scream and felt a pain sharper than she'd ever experienced. One more step and she was on the ground. As she fell she screamed again, realizing that the first guttural wail had been wrenched from her own throat.

"I'm sorry. I couldn't stop. Are you all right?" Nicki couldn't speak past a jaw clenched against the pain shooting up from her right ankle. On her mind was a single thought—there'd be no dancing tonight.

Julian shook hands with his colleagues, tired but glad he'd agreed to the last-minute invite to join a San Francisco symposium on holistic alternatives to traditional remedies for mental illness. Most doctoral students couldn't wait until school was over. But Julian relished the classroom and missed the sometimes passionate discussions around another's point of view. He reached his car, slid inside and fired up the phone. After trying unsuccessfully to use it from several different locations inside during the day, he'd turned it off and placed it inside his briefcase. No hesitation in doing that. Julian lived a life that was consciously predictable. Which was why he was surprised to hear several pings as soon as his phone turned on that indicated missed calls.

He tapped and scrolled. Natalie? Couldn't imagine what she wanted. He'd hired a capable assistant, a forty-seven-year-old single mother named Katie. At their luncheon he'd made it clear to Natalie that he was not in competition with her father, and that she'd provided the only assistance he would ever need from her. There was a call from Katie and one from his mother. The other was from Nicki. He clicked on her number and was surprised to see she'd called multiple times. As he started his car and rolled out of the parking lot, he tapped the steering wheel to engage her number. Ready to leave a message, surprised when she answered the phone.

Confused, he glanced at the dashboard and then at his watch. "Babe, why are you answering the phone? You should be…what's wrong?"

It was after eight on the East Coast. She should be on stage. Something was definitely not right.

"Babe…"

Sniffles and then, "I'm hurt."

"What happened?"

In halting, pain-filled detail, she told him. "Tomorrow I'll see a specialist who'll determine exactly how long I'll be down. I pray that it's only a couple weeks. But it could be longer. Julian, I'm scared. If my ankle is broken, they'll replace me. What am I going to do?"

"You're going to be okay," he replied quickly, his voice calm and firm. "No matter what happens. And you'll come here, to Paradise Cove, so that I can make sure you get the very best care available. So that I can take care of you."

Chapter 5

Julian had factored a good six months into getting his practice up and running with a stream of regular patients. Until that happened, he felt he'd have time on his hands. He'd hired an agent to book college talks and professional speaking engagements. Had set up a schedule with the Drake Community Center's director to offer free counseling to the troubled youth it served. The first month was understandably slow. In August, following an article featuring him in a national medical magazine, he began getting referrals from medical doctors in neighboring towns. Some from as far away as Sacramento and San Jose.

Last week, a former patient of Dr. Johnson had walked into his office. He'd been treated for ten years and felt it wasn't working. At first Julian refused outright, but after a thorough interview, he'd decided to treat the man. People regularly changed therapists. For the patient, the change proved beneficial. For Julian, it had been fateful. The satisfied patient had obviously been talking. Barely into September and a stream of Johnson's patients had called for appointments. He turned most of them down, but agreed to see the ones he felt would benefit from his counsel. One was in his office now, engaging in a pattern most likely developed in childhood and perfected throughout her adult life.

He stole a glance at the clock on the wall behind where his patient Vanessa sat. Nicki's plane would arrive in just over ninety minutes. To leave right now would be cutting it close, and Vanessa's time would be up in sixty seconds. But she was in crisis. He could not in good conscience end the session before her emotions stabilized.

He watched her twist a tissue to shreds as she recounted an incident from her abusive childhood. Tears for moments she'd probably relived thousands of times. It was neither healthy nor productive, but he knew why she did it. Why millions of people relived the very situations they'd most like to forget. How one could at first hate and then—after depression became the new normal and sadness felt sane— relish the pain.

In psychology it was called destiny neurosis, a form of repetition compulsion. The term was coined by Sigmund Freud in 1914 and expanded after further research. As she had during each previous session, Vanessa lamented over the beatings endured at the hands of her parents, and later a foster mom after the parents lost custody, yet was despondent that a physically abusive third marriage was ending. In the past, a cocktail of antianxiety and antidepressant medication had been prescribed as the cure for her chronic depression. Masking the pain, not fixing the problem. Prescription drug abuse was an epidemic in America. Seventy percent of the country was on some type of prescribed drug. A quarter of them were like Vanessa—depressed, abused, hurting. It's one of the reasons Julian had chosen psychology over psychiatry, to push himself toward holistic, drug-free healing and make prescribed medicine the absolute last resort.

"I just want to be loved without being beaten. You know?" She looked at him with red-rimmed eyes. "Is that too much to ask?"

"Not at all, Vanessa. Being beaten is not love. It is what you have come to associate with love, because the abuse you suffered was done by people who said they loved you, those who professed to care about you. Do you understand that?"

"What am I doing wrong, Doctor? How do I keep attracting the same type of man into my life?"

"By repeating the same thought patterns and the same actions that brought you to my office. But that's why I'm here. To help you replace toxic thoughts and actions with positive, productive ones." Julian looked at his watch and stood. "I have a couple things I'd like to give you." He continued talking as he walked over to a wall unit. He pulled a card from a drawer beneath the shelving and a blank journal from a stack on one of the shelves. On the front was a message in large, bold letters: Focus on Good Thoughts and Good Things Will Happen.

He walked back to Vanessa, who had stood as well. "I want you to begin keeping a journal. Every day, write at least one page of what you are thinking. It can be anything, any thought that comes to mind. How you're feeling. How you slept the night before. What you watched on TV or ate for dinner. Doesn't matter. The point is to get in touch with yourself and become conscious of the storyline that's playing in your head."

He held up the five-by-seven card. "Here is a list of questions to help get you started. Your first journal entry can be answering these questions. There are no wrong answers. Just write how you feel."

"But, Doctor—"

"No buts." He took her arm and gently guided her toward the door. "You can do this, Vanessa. It'll help you get better, okay? See you next week."

Traffic was light, and the gods were kind. Forty-five minutes at mostly ninety miles an hour helped him reach the airport within minutes of Nicki's arrival. Jennifer had suggested he send a car service. Much too impersonal for his queen, and for someone who'd experienced a career-threatening injury less than a week ago. He wanted to get her himself.

He parked the car and went inside, hoping she'd take his advice and use a wheelchair instead of trying to navigate the busy airport on crutches. So independent, his private dancer. A trait that over the years had often put them at odds. It had taken less coaxing than expected for her agreement to recuperate in Paradise Cove. And while he'd not promised that the specialist he'd lined up could cut her recovery from six weeks to four, it was a carrot he'd gladly dangled to bring her home.

Once inside he looked at the monitor for her flight number. The plane had landed. Most likely, she was on her way down. He checked his phone. There was a text from his mom.

Dinner with Nicki? Private room @ the club?

He quickly responded. Thanks, Mom. Not tonight.

Sunday brunch?

We'll see.

He looked up just as a set of elevator doors opened. A heavily wrapped ankle supported by an Aircast was the first body part through the doors. It was Nicki, busily texting while the wheelchair assistant pushed her toward baggage claim. Just as she looked up, his phone dinged.

He walked to her, smiling. "Is that a message telling me you've arrived?"

"Yep."

Reaching into his pocket, he pulled out a wad of bills,

peeled off a twenty and tipped the assistant. "Thanks, buddy. I'll take it from here."

"It's okay," Nicki protested. "I can walk."

"Perhaps. But what you will do is accept the generous offer to be ferried in your silver chariot from this building to my car." He leaned down and kissed her scowling lips. "You're welcome. How was the flight?"

"Fine, since I slept through most of it. Doctor gave me pain meds. Can't feel the throbbing ache in my ankle, which is great. But I end up not feeling much of anything else, either." She pointed out a large piece of hard plastic luggage with a colorful strip of material wrapped around the handle. "That's mine."

Julian retrieved it. "How many more?"

"That's it."

"You packed clothes for a four- to six-week stay in one suitcase?"

"You said I'd be treated by the best...what did you call him?"

"An orthopedic specialist."

"Yeah, him."

"Even the most gifted doctor cannot make the body heal faster. Here, you roll the suitcase and I'll roll you."

"If you insist."

"I do."

Julian quickly got Nicki settled into the front seat, and less than an hour from when he'd arrived at Oakland International Airport, they were headed back to PC. With rush-hour traffic waning, he set the cruise control to a law-abiding seventy miles per hour.

"You were supposed to call me last night."

Nicki spoke through a yawn. "Forgot."

"That was disobedient. When we get home, I'm going to have to spank you."

"Lucky me."

Said so sincerely and with such deadpan disinterest that Julian burst out laughing.

"So…what's the official verdict? Broken?"

"Technically, no, and did you know that an actual break or full tear of the ligament and tendons would have been better than the partial tears that I have?"

"I'd heard that before."

"I hadn't. Doesn't make sense that a more serious break would heal faster."

"Life doesn't always make sense."

Nicki fell silent. When they were together, she was usually the more talkative of the two. It was one of her traits that made them such a perfect couple. People didn't recognize how quiet Julian was when he and Nicki were together. The rare occasions when she was quieter than Julian were very obvious. Like now, when the only sound was the neo-soul on Julian's playlist.

He looked over. "You okay?"

She didn't answer right away. While staring out the window she finally replied, "Not really."

"I understand."

Nicki made a skeptical snort. "Please."

"I do, babe."

"You have no idea what I'm going through." Nicki's piercing look was only matched by the ever-increasing volume of her delivery. "How could you? You're not a dancer! You haven't been working toward a dream for well over ten years and then right when you are just about there, so close you can throw a rock and hit it, and thirty years old, something happens that takes it all away. Unless that exact thing has happened to you, there is no way you can relate."

Julian became silent, subconsciously and without thought interpreting the behavior from a professional perspective. Hurt. Fear. Disappointment. Misplaced anger. Nicki had lashed out at him, but her anger was actually toward the situation and the man on the bike who'd instigated it. Fear of the unknown and the unproductive projecting of a worst-case scenario upon an unpredictable situation. Understandable, considering the fickle nature of entertainment. In one day and out the next. That's why he knew better than to comment. There was no right answer for this type of reaction.

The silence lasted through two more songs.

Nicki repositioned her leg. "I hate when you do that."

"What?"

"Psychoanalyze me—and don't deny it. Over there all calm and quiet. I know what you're doing."

"Okay." Said low and drawn out, as if testing the word to see if any repercussions would come along with it.

"Stop!" Nicki punched his arm, but she was smiling. "Is there ever a moment when you're not trying to figure someone out?"

"I can't help being who I am, love."

"I know. I'm sorry."

"You're forgiven. This is a tough time. What did the director say?"

"I was supposed to call him after meeting with the specialist. I decided to wait until I see the doctor that was recommended to you. Do I have an appointment?"

"The earliest I could get you in was this Friday."

"Today is Tuesday." Nicki did a slow exhale. "I'll call tomorrow and ask Milo to wait until Friday to make any… permanent changes. Dammit!" Nicki used her good foot to stomp the floor.

They continued to talk intermittently between Nicki's quiet spells. Knowing she was in no mood to socialize, Julian waited until they were ten minutes outside Paradise

Cove and then called in an order to Acquired Taste for Nicki's favorite meal.

"I have some news that will make you feel a little better."

"What?"

"A place for us to stay."

"You bought a house?"

"I just closed on it. I hope you like it."

"What matters is if you like it. I'm only going to be here for a couple weeks."

"I know, but…you've always been uncomfortable staying at my parents'. So I had Terrell bring me a couple listings. I chose a town house that resembles a brownstone on the inside."

She gave him a look.

"On the inside, I said!" He reached over and took her hand. "I know that no place will ever come close to your beloved Brooklyn or Manhattan. But I want to make you as comfortable and happy as I can while you're here."

"Ah, that's sweet, babe."

"I do have to warn you about something."

"What?"

"I just got it, so it's pretty empty."

"I'm sure I can make it work."

"Just letting you know."

They arrived at the echoing town house a short time later. A sectional sofa was the living room's lone furniture. The master suite was also sparsely furnished, its major feature a king-size bed. Julian helped Nicki shower, tucked her in bed, then joined her there with two tray tables. They watched TV while enjoying burgers and fries. Once the trays were removed and they'd finished their drinks, Julian pulled back the covers and raised the short nightie that covered the shaved lips that he so adored. The good food, hot shower and crisp clean sheets had been arranged with the intention to make Nicki more comfortable. Now it was time to make both of them happy.

Chapter 6

A steady throb served as her alarm clock. The ache forced her eyes open as she slowly floated up from a pain medication—induced fog. Her eyes flickered against bright sunlight and over to the digital clock on a nightstand. Ten o'clock? No way. She fell back against the pillows, but the cry for relief from the ache that went from the tear in her ankle to her shin would not be denied.

She threw back the covers and hobbled into the en suite bath. Her toiletry bag was set next to one of two brass-and-glass vessel sinks that contrasted beautifully against light-colored granite and ebony cabinets. A note was stuck on the mirror above it. Had he emptied her suitcase? What else had she slept through?

She read the extensive note, written in his neat, slanted penmanship.

Morning, beautiful. You slept so peacefully as I prepared to leave I hadn't the heart to wake you. Breakfast is in the fridge, a credit card on the table. Please go online and order whatever you feel will make the town house a home. For ideas, call Mom. For company, call Quinn. Both cannot wait to see you. Or not—your choice. The main thing is to feel better. Restaurant choices don't compare to Times Square but all deliver. Call when you read this. Loving you…

She looked down and noticed that beside her toiletry bag was a bottle of water. So naturally thoughtful. Innately kind. Julian had always treated her wonderfully, with the sweetest adoration and the deepest respect. Hard to admit, but sometimes she took it for granted. It had taken a break and a few dates with Vince to remind her how good she had it, how special Julian was. And here he was showing her again.

She took a pain pill. After a quick shower during which she more than appreciated the double shower's built-in bench, Nicki wrapped a fresh bandage around her ankle, slipped on a loose mini and the Aircast and after a last-minute hop back to grab her cell, made her way downstairs with the aid of one crutch. She hadn't felt hungry, but a growling stomach let her know that nourishment was needed.

She opened the fridge and pulled out the lone white sack that sat next to bottles of water, orange and cranberry juices, and a variety of flavored coffees. She opened one of the coffees and drank almost half of it with the first swig. Inside the bag were pastries, a bagel and a breakfast sandwich. Forgetting Julian's warning, she opened a cabinet door to grab a plate. The cupboard was literally bare. She improvised a plate from the top of the paper container, scooped out the sandwich's insides and nuked them in the microwave.

While reassembling the sandwich it came to her. The reason she'd tossed and turned last night. The feeling of isolation she'd felt that morning. She slowly looked around the room and wondered if she'd ever before experienced life quite this way. No noise. Total silence. So quiet she felt she could hear herself think.

For a woman who'd grown up in the hustle and bustle of Prospect Heights, with traffic and trains, the conversation of close neighbors floating through her window, and a dozen other sounds, the quiet was strange, almost eerie. She rapped a line from the musical. Her voice bounced against the walls, evaporated into the eighteen-foot vaulted ceiling.

Last night she'd barely noticed, but against the bright

morning, the beauty of the home's architecture stood out. Tan-colored ceilings and Tasmanian oak floors were a nice and different accent against ivory walls and complemented an ultramodern, dual-stone fireplace that served both the living and dining rooms. Chandeliers, modern fixtures and recessed lighting all added to the home's warm yet sophisticated style.

Nice, she thought. Who was she kidding? The place was beyond nice. It was stunning. Like those she viewed in magazines and fantasized about owning. What was its value, she wondered. In Brooklyn such a home would go for two or three million. In Manhattan, five at least.

She reached the sofa, settled against the soft cashmere cushion and looked around her, thinking she could get used to a luxury lifestyle. Then she remembered why she was here. Not in New York. What the freak bicycle accident might cost her. The bright mood quickly faded.

Just as she was about to head to a pity party, her phone rang. She answered and put the call on speaker.

"Hey, babe."

"Good morning, love. How are you?"

"I'm okay."

"Did you get my note?"

"Uh-huh."

"Then why haven't you called me, as the note instructed?"

"Listen, Doctor..."

The sound of Julian's chuckle made her smile. "I knew that would rile you. My next appointment is due any minute, but I wanted to let you know that Quinn might be calling you. She asked and I gave her your number. Hope you don't mind."

"No, that's fine. I hadn't planned to get out, but after coming downstairs and seeing how empty this place really is, I might not have a choice. At the very least we need dishes and silverware."

"And towels. The two hanging in the bathroom are the only two in the house."

"Oh my God."

"Hey, I tried. It was either an empty house for just us or a fully furnished wing at my parents' house."

"I appreciate what you did for me, babe. This place is beautiful."

"Katie's calling. Appointment's here. Love you."

Nicki eased off the couch and took her now-empty containers into the kitchen to throw away. Not used to having downtime, she felt strangely out of sorts with so much of it now on her hands. A plan, that's it. A plan and a few projects. That's what she thought could help the time go quickly until her foot healed and she was back on stage in New York, where she belonged.

Back on the couch, she pressed the note icon on her phone and began to make a list. First: find a yoga studio. Nicki couldn't dance or put pressure on her ankle, but a yoga class, especially hot yoga, would help her stay limber and maybe even help her ankle heal, too. What else? Furnish Julian's house. That project alone could take four weeks. Four bedrooms—three unfurnished—three bathrooms, combined living/dining space and a patio, too? She'd keep it clean and simple, safe earth colors, Julian's style. But on what kind of budget? Sure, the black card on the table had no monetary limits, but did Julian? Did she? It had taken her almost a year to personalize her two-bedroom walkup. Just as a sense of anxiety began to creep in, her phone rang.

"Hello?"

"Nicki! It's Quinn. I'm so sorry for what happened to you!"

"Thanks, Quinn. I'm pretty bummed about it."

"I can't even imagine how you're feeling. You were so great in the show. Several scenes with the lead. Sold-out crowds."

"Hey, I don't need reminding."

"You're right. I'm…stupid and inconsiderate is what I am. Would you believe I was calling to cheer you up?"

"Ha! You meant well."

"How's the ankle?"

"Still swollen. Still throbbing."

"Is it broken?"

"Worse, the ligaments are torn and the tendons are ruptured. The doctor said a clean break would have healed faster."

"Tell you what. Why don't I come grab you, show you around our cosmopolitan…uh, town."

"I'm glad you didn't say city."

"I started to, but the lie wouldn't come out of my mouth. I don't know if you're up for it, but I knew you were here and wanted to offer."

"That's nice of you, Quinn. I didn't think I'd be up for much socializing, but I need to hear something besides my thoughts. I'm so used to having noise around me that the quiet feels claustrophobic."

"Totally understand. When I first moved from San Francisco, I thought I'd go small-town crazy! Is a half hour enough time for you to be ready?"

"Just casual, right?"

"Absolutely."

"Do you know where I am?"

"Yes, got the address from Julian."

"Okay, see you then."

Nicki checked the weather. Projection was high seventies. About the same as New York this time of year. Fall was her favorite month in the city. Perfect temps. Changing leaves. She ignored the stab of pain in her heart. Found where Julian had placed the clothes he'd unpacked from her luggage and threw on a pair of wide-legged pants—easiest to navigate around the heavy bandage and Aircast—and a fitted knit top that showed off her toned, flat stomach. A light jacket and bulky wooden jewelry completed the ensemble.

Quinn rang the doorbell moments after Nicki managed to get back downstairs. They walked outside to a sleek red Ferrari.

Nicki's mouth was agape. "This is you?"

Quinn smiled as she tapped the key fob. "Christmas present."

Nicki slid into the seat, folded the crutches and gingerly pulled her injured ankle inside. Seconds later they were out the driveway and zooming down the quiet residential street.

"Wow, this car is something!"

"You like it?"

"Not for me, but it fits you perfectly."

"I can see you behind the wheel."

"I barely even know how to drive, so that wouldn't be a good look."

"You're kidding!"

"I've got my license but not a car. You don't really need one in New York."

"I think not having a car would drive me crazy."

They reached one of the main thoroughfares of Paradise Cove, the one that ran north to south through the city.

"This tour is going to take all of ten minutes, so don't blink."

"I've been here before."

"Oh, really?"

"Yep."

"How long have you and Julian dated?"

"Almost six years, off and on."

"That's a long time, Nicki. Do you think you two will get married?"

"I don't know. He asked me once, but…"

"You turned him down?" Disbelief took Quinn's voice up a notch.

"I know. Sometimes I can't believe it, either." Nicki sighed. "I love Julian. He's a really good guy. But he's California, and I'm New York. I can't see myself living here, and I know this is where he wants to be."

"I said the same thing. Was only supposed to be here six months. But now? I love it. When I want a dose of the big city, I go to one. But I like coming back to the relative peace of a small town. Even more, I love being married to Ike. No city in the world can compare to having a Drake man love you."

"You're probably right. But after turning him down the first time, I doubt that he'll ask again."

They reached the town square.

"Ooh. What's that?"

"On the corner? That's London's store. Hang on." Quinn whipped around, barely slowing down. The car fishtailed, but she broke right hard and pulled into one of several empty parking spaces available on the quiet morning.

Nicki slowly released the death grip her fingers had on the dash. "I just saw my life pass in front of me."

"That scare you? Don't worry. I know what I'm doing."

"Maybe, but while I'm riding can we practice safety first so that my ankle remains the only thing broken?"

Quinn laughed. "Sure, come on."

"Where are we going?"

"You don't want to go inside?"

"Since getting here nearly cost me my life, I guess I could. Is this London as in—"

"Yes, that London. Oh, wait. Your foot. I forgot just that quickly. We can go another day."

"I'm hoping the specialist will tell me that my PC days are numbered. Let's go in. I won't be able to walk around much. But I'd like to see her shop."

"You can sit and I'll bring over stuff that I think you'll like."

"Okay."

A chime sounded as Quinn opened the door. Inside, the color of the walls grabbed Nicki's attention right away. She would have thought textured black wallpaper too dark for a retail establishment. But a white ceiling and bright lights everywhere gave the expansive room a runway vibe. Uniquely designed separates in bold prints, like the ones in the display that had caught Nicki's eye, adorned the walls and clothes racks. Mirrors abounded. Music with an alternative sound was a nice yet unobtrusive companion to one's shopping experience. Despite her plan to sit and be pampered, Nicki was drawn to minimally filled racks of clothing that were just her style. Of the garments she'd seen so far, she wanted them all.

A pretty young woman came from behind the retro counter made of stainless steel. The door chimed again. Two more women entered. One honed in on her target and made a beeline for Nicki.

"It is you?"

"Excuse me?"

"Nicki Long?"

"Yes," she said slowly, cautiously.

"I told my friend it was you! What happened to your foot? Is that why you're here and not on Broadway?"

It was the very thing Nicki knew she wouldn't like about small towns—everyone trying to be in her business.

"Just a sprain."

"Oh, thank goodness. So you'll be back in the show soon."

"That's the plan."

"My mom and I are trying to get tickets. We're thinking about going over the Thanksgiving holiday. Hey, is it possible for me to get a picture with you?"

"Sure."

The woman waved over her friend, who took the phone and snapped the picture.

"Thank you!"

"You're welcome. What's your name?"

"Ashley," Quinn interrupted. "The local gossip trying to break news like that celebrity news show, *XYZ.* Writes a blog gossiping about everything she thinks she knows. You're guaranteed to be on it tomorrow." Quinn's eyes shifted to Ashley. "Right?"

"You got it! Just ask Ashley!" She turned to Nicki. "That's my blog, *Ask Ashley.*" Then to Quinn. "I take exception to your description of my popular blog. *Gossip* implies that what I write isn't true."

"Most of it isn't."

"Clearly a matter of opinion." Ashley's smile at Nicki was genuine. "It was really great to meet you." And to Quinn, "Always a pleasure. Bye, ladies. Come on, Nat. Let's go."

Quinn watched her go, shaking her head. "She's so fake."

"Wouldn't know it to look at her. She seemed nice to me."

"Bright smile. Dark heart."

"Wow, what'd she do to you?"

"Not to me. To Niko. Ask Julian about it. I don't want her messiness to junk up our day."

Chapter 7

Julian pulled into his driveway and parked the car. Kept it out of the garage in case Nicki wanted to go out to dinner. He walked up the town house steps, pulling out his phone to check the text message that had just come in.

Who's Ashley?

He read it and frowned, called out to Nicki as he came in the door.

"Nicki! Babe?"

"Up here."

He walked upstairs. Nicki sat against the headboard, checking her phone. "Ashley who?" was his greeting as he walked over to the bed, kissed her forehead and sat down.

"The one Quinn doesn't like."

"Ah. That Ashley. So you did get out."

"Yes, Quinn came by. Took me around town, driving like a maniac."

"That sounds like her."

"We went by London's store. It's nice."

"That's where you ran into Ashley?"

Nicki nodded. "She and another woman came in right after we did. Who is she?"

"Somebody we grew up with—my older brothers, really. A lot of guys dated her. She had a crush on Niko that bordered on obsession."

"He dated her, too?"

"They messed around. When he met Monique, things got a little crazy. Ashley tried to sabotage the situation. But everything worked out."

"She asked for a selfie. Quinn said I'd probably be on her blog. Have you read it?"

"I checked out a couple things she wrote about—mostly fluff pieces. Gossip. She probably will write about you. A Broadway performer in our little hamlet—why wouldn't she? But I don't think you have anything to worry about." He glanced at his phone, tapped the screen and shook his head. "It must be the day for silliness."

"Somebody sent you a nonsense text?"

"When I let you go earlier, thinking my client had arrived? Wasn't my client. It was an old classmate named Natalie Moore."

"Classmate or girlfriend?"

"What did I say?"

"I heard what you said. I'm getting clarity on what you meant."

He reached for her hand, kissed it. "A classmate who I hadn't seen for years, since I was fifteen, sixteen years old. Anyway, to find an assistant, I signed up with a local staffing agency. Turns out she owns it."

"Didn't you hire an assistant?"

"Yes."

"Then why is she coming to your office?"

"It's a long story." Julian removed his shoes, sat against the headboard beside her and told her about the earlier encounter.

Julian had just pulled up a patient's file when his intercom buzzed. "Yes, Katie."

"Doctor, Natalie Moore is here to see you."

Natalie? What did she want? "Is my eleven o'clock here?"

"Not yet."

"Okay. I'll…" He looked up as his door opened. Natalie

sauntered in on four-inch heels, balancing her petite frame like a pro on stilts. When they'd met for lunch, she'd worn a suit and her hair in a loose bun, and aside from a flirtation or two, their interaction had been totally professional. Today the thick mane of brunette curls cascaded over her shoulders and down her back.

Julian's calm belied his ire. "Natalie, what are you doing?"

"Don't worry. I won't be long."

Hopefully as short as her skirt. If someone came to an interview in the tight mini she wore today it would be totally inappropriate, along with her behavior of entering his office without being invited and sitting down before being asked.

"Had you waited, I would have asked Katie to schedule you an appointment, the same as others who need to speak with me."

"Oh, Julian, don't be so formal. I heard you have a patient coming. Is it another one of my dad's?"

"Is that why you're here?"

"That's part of it. Dad has lost several since you've opened your office. What are you doing, offering a grand opening sale? Or is it the disparaging comments you've made about doctors as drug pushers that have patients leaving him to darken your door?"

"Natalie, my practice doesn't concern you. Why are you so interested in it?"

"Why are you evading my questions?"

"I'm not doing this with you. Your father's a grown man. If he has questions, he can ask them. As for the formalities of this office, they are there for a reason. We grew up together, but those interactions were a long time ago. We were children, and this is not school. If you need professional help in the future, make an appointment. Am I clear?"

"No need to be rude, Julian." Natalie rose from the chair and started for the door. "My dad has too much class to confront you, but let me be clear. People are watching. They see my dad's clients coming to this building, some who have been with him for years. What you're doing is unethical. And I'm going to find a way to expose it."

Julian stood. He'd had enough.

"I'm leaving. But you've been warned."

"Warned? What did she mean by that?"

Julian realized sharing with Nicki what had happened earlier might not have been the best idea. Her fiery nature was one of the things he loved about her. That she didn't sugarcoat or hide her feelings was a plus, too—most of the time. Might not be particularly advantageous while living in a small town. If Nicki met Natalie after what he'd just told her, it might not go so well.

"I don't know what she meant. But whatever it is means nothing to me." He spoke lightheartedly, adding a smile to further convey his nonchalance. "Let's talk about what's really important. You, and how you're feeling. Better, I'd imagine, since you went out."

"The ankle is still pretty painful, unless I'm taking the meds. Which I don't like taking because they knock me out. That's why your cabinets and pantry are still bare and dinner isn't ready."

"You'd planned to do all of that today?"

"It was a good plan in my head."

"What about now? Feel like going out to eat?"

"Would you be all right having something delivered?"

Julian ran his hand across her thigh, slid it between her legs and let it rest near her mound. "If I do, what's in it for me?"

"You mean…" Nicki's eyelids dropped, her voice, too, becoming low and sexy. "Besides a sandwich?"

Julian tried to hide it, but a smile escaped and grew as he chuckled. "It's good to see you happy."

"I'm hopeful about my appointment with the specialist on Friday, and the chance that he'll have good news. You can still take me, right?"

"Of course. What if he agrees with your New York doctor and you have to be out for four to six weeks?"

"Then I'll probably get replaced, and that will not make me happy." Nicki's shoulders slumped.

"Let's hope for the best and see what happens." Julian stole a quick kiss and slid off the bed. "What are you in the mood for? Italian, American, Mexican, Chinese?"

"Whatever you're having is fine with me."

"What I want most on the menu is you."

"Whatever."

"I'm going to take a shower. Order something for both of us." He turned on the water and quickly undressed. Under the pulsating jets and the hot water, the knots in his neck and shoulders began to dissipate. She'd answered dismissively, but Julian knew his comment made her wet. Or at the very least caused a little squiggle. In the six off-and-on years of their relationship, he'd studied Nicki as diligently as he had his textbooks. How to please her. What made her smile. Being on stage, performing, was one of those things. If Friday's prognosis knocked her out of the show, Julian didn't have a cure to fix it. The situation with Natalie was another matter. He hoped today was the end of her bothersome antics and threats to his practice. Because this wasn't school, and he wouldn't be bullied. If she pushed, Natalie would see that Julian had grown into a man well able to take care of his woman, and himself.

Chapter 8

Friday morning, Nicki was nervous. She hadn't slept well last night, and when Julian offered to leave early and have breakfast she declined. Her stomach was in knots. She couldn't eat a thing. They headed to San Jose and the specialist who'd see Nicki, forty-five minutes away. On the drive, Julian tried to lift her spirits by reminding her of what was planned for after the appointment. The event for which London and Ace had been planning, New York Fashion Week, was in full swing. Later, she and Julian, along with most of the Drake family, were flying over to attend Ace's show. London was walking the runway for her husband's line. But even returning to the city she loved was filled with mixed emotions. How would it feel to be in New York if she'd been replaced in the show?

They reached Dr. Allen's office just before the 10:00 a.m. appointment. Nicki refused Julian's offer to help her out of the car, as if maneuvering on her own would bring her one step closer to healing. She'd filled out the patient paperwork online, so once they were inside, the cheery receptionist quickly directed Nicki and Julian to the inner offices. A medical assistant took Nicki's vitals and several digital photos of her ankle before escorting her into another room to take X-rays. Minutes later Nicki rejoined Julian back in the examination room. Not long after that, the doctor came in. He was younger than Nicki imagined he'd be, but his deep blue eyes were piercing and kind.

"Good morning, Nicki, sorry to keep you waiting. I'm Dr. Allen." He shook Julian's hand as well. "I hear you're a dancer."

"Yes, that's why I'm really anxious to hear what you've

got to say about the X-rays. I'm in a show right now—or I was until the accident—a show that has a good chance for a long run on Broadway. So I'm hoping you have good news."

"No news yet. Let's take a look. If I can have you sit up there for me." He motioned to the elevated hospital bed. "Here, let me help you."

Both he and Julian assisted Nicki to her feet. She took a couple hops over to the bed and perched on it. "Do I need to lie down?"

"No, you're fine. Let me get a look at that ankle."

Dr. Allen sat on a stool with wheels and rolled up to where he was eye level with Nicki's extended leg. He placed one hand under her leg to support it and used the other to gingerly touch her ankle in various places. "It's still quite swollen," he observed. "Have you kept it elevated as much as possible?"

"I don't remember the other doctor telling me to elevate it. But I have spent a considerable amount of time in bed, so…"

"That's not the same. The foot needs to be elevated when sitting and also when lying down by using pillows to place it higher than your head. The deep bruising here—" he pointed to an area on the right side of her ankle "—and here—" his finger continued to midshin "—causes me the greatest concern. They allude to the possibility of damage beyond a major sprain." He swiveled his chair around, reached for a remote and pressed a button. What looked like a simple whiteboard was actually a projector with the X-rays of Nicki's foot and ankle now on display.

Reaching into the pocket of his white jacket, he pulled out a pointer and rolled closer to the screen, identifying certain areas as he spoke. "To isolate the injuries and causes of pain, I checked both the medial and lateral ankle, the base of the fifth metatarsal, the Lisfranc region—that's right here—and the medial, lateral and posterior tendons. I also checked the syndesmosis—that's the area back here by the heel, for stability—and the fibula. There are signs of stress but no significant tearing. Which is good. The bruising on the side of your ankle that concerned me is due to an avulsion fracture, which means a small piece of bone has separated from the main mass of bone that is connected to this tendon." He ran the pointer down a long, thick line within several others.

Julian leaned forward, studying the screen. "That sounds more serious than a grade-two sprain, Doctor."

"It is."

"What does that mean?" Nicki didn't try to hide her rising anxiety. "Will I have to have surgery?"

"I don't want to recommend treatment based on these radiographs alone, so I have ordered an MRI to provide a more definitive image."

Nicki's eyes widened. "You mean go inside that tube thingy?"

Dr. Allen smiled. "No, Nicki. We have a scanner that functions without you having to be fully enclosed."

Her relief was evident. "How soon can we do that?"

"As soon as we can get you down there."

"And how long for the results?" Julian asked.

"Hopefully by Monday."

"Is there any way they can come sooner? I told the director of my stage production that I'd have an answer today about how long it will take for my ankle to heal."

Again the slight smile that Nicki realized was more from habit than anything else. "Unfortunately we cannot get MRI results back in less than twenty-four hours. But I think it's safe to say you won't be out for more than four weeks."

"Four weeks! Doctor, I can't."

"Perhaps less if the MRI reveals that the bone isn't actually fractured. Even then, it will be at least a week before you can begin physical therapy and at least two weeks to fully heal. You being in shape as a dancer is helpful. It will speed your recovery. I wish I had better news, but we don't want you to go back to work prematurely and risk permanent injury. In the meantime, keep the foot elevated when possible. Pay attention to the swelling, which should go down considerably in the next couple days. Also begin testing the ankle, gently, for its flexibility and level of pain."

Julian stood as the doctor did, holding out his hand. "Thanks, Doctor."

"You're welcome." He walked over to Nicki. "Chin up, Nicki. As bad as this is, when it comes to bicycle accidents I've seen much worse."

"Thank you, Dr. Allen."

"I'm happy to help. Someone will be in shortly to take you down for the MRI. After that, you're free to go. I'll call you on Monday as soon as there's news."

Back in the car, Nicki wasn't happy, and not even Julian's positive perspective could cheer her up.

"Look at the good side, babe. Not getting this second opinion could have led to permanent damage. This way you heal correctly, and come back at one hundred percent."

"Come back to what? Auditions for another marginal play or the rigors of regional theater and months on the road in a tour bus? Like I've done off and on for the last seven years? With that role in *A Hair's Tale*, I thought those days were over." She dug through her purse, mumbling, "Looks like the only thing that's over is my part in it."

She pulled out her phone, scrolled through the contact list and tapped the screen.

"Who are you calling?"

"Milo, the director."

"Sure that can't wait until Monday, when you have news?"

"Probably." When Milo's voice mail answered, she hung up without leaving a message. "It'll be better to talk to him then, anyway, and tell him I'll be back dancing in three weeks or less."

"I know that's what you want, babe. But best not to get your hopes up until you have more information."

"I'm just being positive, like you said. You did say that, right?"

"You're right. I did. Just don't want you to be disappointed."

"I'm going to make sure of that myself. Where there's a will, there's a way, and one way or another, a couple weeks from Monday, I'll be back on that stage."

Her mind might have doubted, but Nicki's voice was strong and filled with conviction. Misdiagnoses happened. Doctors had been wrong before. Nicki hadn't come this far to let a tiny bone fragment stop her. Tickets continued to be sold out. The show got rave reviews. There was a sense of certainty in her gut. *A Hair's Tale* was going to have a long run on Broadway. And so was she.

Chapter 9

When they'd first met, Nicki found Julian's wealth intimidating. So he'd downplayed it. As she watched the private jet's stairs transform into a ramp that could accommodate the wheelchair upon which he'd insisted, even she admitted money had its privileges.

Once on board the sleek Challenger 850, her appreciation continued. The stark brightness of the cabin with its white walls and ceiling was complemented perfectly by the black flooring, dark gray leather seats and various shades of gray that continued throughout. Splashes of red interrupted the black, white and gray theme, just enough to bring interest to the palette without lessening the sophistication of the cabin's smart design.

Nicki immediately thought of the town house and its similar color scheme and wondered if they'd been remodeled by the same designer. The wheelchair was folded and stored up front. Nicki had no problem using her crutches to navigate the aisle. It was one reason Julian had wanted to arrive early, before the plane's fourteen seats were totally filled. And according to him, they would be. They bypassed two rows of forward-facing chairs and a meeting area with chairs facing each other and a love seat between them. Across from the meeting area was a full bathroom, complete with a marble shower. Beyond that were tables on either side of the aisle framed by two sets of chairs. Perfect for dining or playing games. Nicki directed Julian to the chairs facing the front. He then reached into one of the overhead bins and pulled out a couple pillows to place under her ankle and elevate it, as Dr. Allen had instructed.

Nicki turned the chair so that Julian could place her leg on the pillows on the chair beside her.

"How is that? Are you comfortable?"

"Yes, that's fine."

"Are you sure? Is it hurting? Do you need to take some medication?"

"It's throbbing a little, but I don't want to take anything."

The flight attendant came over. "Dr. Drake, could I get you or your guest something to drink or a snack?"

Julian looked at Nicki, who shook her head. He sat across from her. "No, thank you. We're fine for now."

"This is my first time on a private plane, and I can't believe how different it looks from regular ones. With love seats and tables, a full bath! It's more beautiful and well appointed than most homes I've been to. And here I've thought myself big-time when paying fifty extra bucks to upgrade for more leg room! After this trip, flying regular will never be the same." She looked at him, her face a question. "Is this how you fly when we're not together?"

"No, and it's not the way any other of the family flies all the time, either. This is the company plane, used almost exclusively for company business. On some occasions the paths of business and pleasure cross and the plane can be used to accommodate both."

"But you usually fly first-class."

"So do you when you're with me."

"I know."

"So what's your point?"

"I guess I forget sometimes how rich you are."

Julian turned to face her fully. "I'll tell you what my dad told me when I was younger. He's rich. We kids used borrowed money that came from the rich dad."

"Thanks for trying to be humble, but you're rich, too."

"My financial portfolio is healthy. But it wasn't all

handed to me. My parents gave me a good foundation that I've worked hard to build on."

A sudden din of voices announced the next group's arrival. Nicki looked up as Julian's sister Teresa and her husband, Atka, entered, joking with Niko, Monique and their pregnant sister-in-law Charli, followed by Terrell.

Julian stood as the couples waved and sat, all except Niko and Terrell, who continued toward them. "Wow, Niko. Back-to-back New York trips in less than a month? London's got clout."

"She must not be the only one," Terrell interrupted, "because one glance and everyone knows you're not into fashion."

Julian responded to the good-natured ribbing with a fake punch to his brother's gut.

"How are you, Nicki?" Terrell leaned over for a hug. "Sure you're able to be in New York and not get on stage?"

"Not at all."

"We can't have you trying to dance before that ankle is ready. Julian, you'd better watch her."

"I'm on it, bro. Don't worry. Where's Aliyah?"

"She had to work."

"And she let you roll solo?"

Terrell put a finger to his lips. "I snuck out the house. Don't tell anyone."

They laughed as Ike Sr. and Jennifer entered the plane along with Ike Jr., Quinn and another couple.

"Who's that?" Julian asked.

"That's Quinn's dad and stepmother. You don't remember them from the wedding?"

"Obviously not."

"Don't even know your own kin," Terrell joked, shaking his head.

"There were almost three hundred people there when

Ike and Quinn got married." Julian looked not one bit embarrassed.

"True, but only one set of parents for Quinn."

"And your point is?"

"That you're stupid," Terrell deadpanned.

Julian looked at Nicki. "See what I had to endure growing up?"

"All that IQ going to waste, being squeezed into forgetfulness inside that small head."

"Brother, I'm concerned. Have you been treated?"

"For what?"

"For the oral acid malabsorption causing diarrhea of the mouth."

"Very funny, Doctor," Terrell said, not laughing.

"Cut it out, you two," Nicki warned. "You're lucky to have each other."

Terrell looked confused. Julian explained, "The misplaced longings of an only child."

"Ah, got it." And then to Nicki. "Come spend a week with all of us together. We'll change your mind."

Quinn brought back her parents, introduced them to Nicki and reacquainted them with Julian. They then joined Ike in the area with the love seat.

"They going to the show?" Julian asked Terrell, now joined by his sister-in-law Charli, Atka and Teresa, all sitting at the table across the aisle.

He shook his head. "Handling some East Coast business. Just bumming a ride."

"Nice to have friends in high places," Nicki said.

"Not friends, family," Terrell corrected. "They've only got it like that because Quinn is a Drake."

The flight took off, the group settled in and for the next five hours, Nicki observed and enjoyed some of the undeniable advantages of being a Drake. Besides the private plane and the attendant's stellar service. Dinner was like that from a Michelin-starred chef. Salmon flown in fresh from Atka's Alaskan fishery, lobster tails from Maine. Alkaline water, top-shelf drinks and a cheesecake ice cream with a hot fudge and pecan drizzle that was so decadent and delicious Nicki wanted to lick the bowl.

Even better than the luxury, service and food was the obvious love shared between all of the family. Everyone made sure Nicki felt at home. One by one they came back, said hello and asked how she was doing. Jennifer made a date for them to do lunch the following week. Although Nicki hadn't talked much with Ike Sr.—his presence was very commanding—his greeting was warm, his smile sincere. There was nonstop teasing. Nicki laughed till she cried. And between the couples lots of subtle affection—touches, hand holding, a quick kiss or two. Growing up it had just been her and her mother. Other than in movies, Nicki was sure that she'd never seen true love such as this. She thought about how she'd turned down Julian's proposal and Paige's reaction when she told her. How she'd said no to marrying a smart, wealthy, well-mannered man with values, who came from a loving, close-knit family filled with successful businessmen and celebrities. It seemed like a good idea at the time, but now turning him down felt like the worst mistake she'd ever made. In life, some things only came around once. As they neared her favorite city and the plane began its descent, Nicki felt sure that Julian proposing to her was one of those things.

Chapter 10

There were some things that money—even a lot of it—couldn't buy. Like one's way out of a traffic jam on the Triborough Bridge caused by an accident blocking all lanes. While the women attended the fashion show, the men were headed to a business meeting/national strategy session/fund-raiser for Niko's senatorial campaign. Julian was calm, as usual. His brothers? Not as much. Ike Jr. and Atka talked business, but after every few sentences they'd bring up the delay. Terrell fidgeted. Niko constantly checked his watch. Ike Sr. exchanged trivialities with Quinn's father, Glen.

During a break in their conversation, Julian tapped his dad. "I have a question."

"Yes, son?"

"How familiar are you with Claude Johnson?"

"The psychiatrist?" Julian nodded. Ike Sr. shrugged. "About as familiar as I am with most people in Paradise Cove who've lived there most of their lives. Chatted at a few chamber meetings, maybe a couple times at the club. Fortunately haven't had the need to schedule an appointment yet." Ike Sr. chuckled. Julian smiled. "Why do you ask?"

Julian told his dad about Natalie's visit and accusations. "It's almost as if she's trying to create the illusion of something that isn't there, like I'm purposely trying to sabotage her father's practice."

"Is it true? Have some of his patients left his practice and come to you?"

"Yes, but not enough to warrant her egregious attacks."

Ike Sr. rubbed his jaw, his eyes narrowing as he pondered the situation. "I do recall some type of scandal a while back involving one of his patients. Jennifer most likely could fill in the details. That woman has a way of knowing just about everything that goes on in our town. Junior." Ike Jr. looked over with brow raised. "Do you remember what happened with Claude Johnson around four or five years ago?"

"The doctor?" Ike Jr. asked.

"He was charged with writing fake prescriptions. Supplying medication beyond the scope of his practice to patients he barely treated and some not at all," Niko said.

"Unfortunately, that's a lucrative market," Terrell said. "On the streets, some can pay as much as thirty dollars a pill."

"How do you know anything about him?" Ike Jr. asked Niko. Ike Sr. looked as if he wanted to know that, too. In fact, every eye in the limo was now trained on the mayor. "That I know about it is only a fluke. The attorney who helped squash the story and clean up the mess is married to Greg's sister."

"The city's finance director?" Ike Sr. asked.

Niko nodded. "Small world."

Julian asked the question on everyone's mind. "What happened?"

"Ultimately, the case got thrown out. The main pieces of evidence were obtained illegally, without the proper search warrant. He got written up on some lesser action but was allowed to keep his license. Obviously."

"So that's why," Julian mused.

"Why what?" Niko and the rest hadn't heard what Julian had shared with his father.

Julian shook his head. "Nothing."

"Why his daughter is upset that Julian has opened a practice in town," Ike Sr. shared.

"No, she's probably upset at not getting more alimony." Said without even looking up as Terrell texted on his phone.

"I asked about that, at least indirectly. Commented on the fact that she was married, given the new last name, and that she'd moved back to PC. All she said about her divorce was that it was a long story."

"From what I heard, when it comes to the telling, looks like her husband won. But she came back and opened a business. Can't be doing too bad. Where'd you run into her, Julian? And with all the work you're putting into your own practice, when did you have the time?"

"Irony. Went online and did a search for staffing companies. Contacted the one that was in PC. Wasn't until they called back and I recognized her voice that I learned it was Natalie's company."

"That's right, you would know her. She was a year behind me and one ahead of you."

"Yep."

"I'd be careful around her if I were you," Terrell cautioned. "She might be trying to set up a lawsuit and get some Drake dollars to supplement her income."

Julian nodded and remained quiet as the conversation shifted and traffic on the bridge began to move faster. He was already one step ahead of Terrell. Because when it came to caution regarding Natalie Moore, his brother hadn't said nothing but a word.

She'd never seen anything like it. The glitz. The glam. Bright lights and beautiful people. She'd spent her whole life in New York, liked clothes as much as the next girl. Had passed by the Fashion Institute of Technology dozens of times and shopped Fifth Avenue stores. But she'd never before considered the actual world of fashion. From where she sat, it was as dazzling, entertaining and fun as a Broadway show.

From the third row of an old synagogue, among a crowd that was standing room only, Nicki took in the high-tech fashion show. Neon lasers, pulsating music and plastic shaped into clothing and made to look like stained glass set the tone for Ace Montgomery's second offering of women's wear called OTB Her. OTB stood for Out of the Box. She remembered that from last year's billboards of London plastered all over town. That was when he'd introduced a collection for women, with London being the face for his line. Now, as then, she commanded the show. Any doubters need look no further than the show's finale. London wore a beautifully painted stained-glass maxi that lit up on the runway when she reached midway. The crowd's cheers turned to roars when she spun to reveal glass shoes that lit up as well.

Backstage was a crush. Quinn and Teresa walked on each side of Nicki as she moved toward the crowd surrounding London as quickly as her crutches would allow. When London saw her family, she pushed through reporters and fans and other celebrities to greet them.

"You were wonderful," Nicki said as London gave her a big hug. "I can't believe I've missed out on this my whole life!"

"You've never been to fashion week?" London asked.

"Never."

"Well, you haven't missed out on anything like what you saw tonight. What Ace is bringing to the fashion world hasn't been done before."

"Ace, how much do you pay her to say things like that?" Julian asked.

Nicki turned and saw that Ace had walked up behind them. She remembered the underwear ads from his modeling days and being in awe of him like the rest of her friends.

Back then she'd never imagined seeing him in person, much less meeting the handsome star. Even if she'd stayed in touch and could tell her high school friends the truth, they probably wouldn't believe it. As good as he looked in magazines, he looked even better in person.

"Ace Montgomery," he said, holding out his hand.

"Wait, y'all haven't met?" London looked between the two.

"No."

"Never."

"What about the family reunion?"

"I was only there a day, remember?" Nicki responded.

"What about...oh, never mind. Babe, this is Julian's girlfriend, Nicki Long. Nicki, Ace Montgomery."

"As though he needs introducing at his very own show," Teresa joked.

"Your clothes are amazing," Nicki said. "Have you thought of designing for Broadway?"

Jennifer had been talking with another of the models but overheard this comment and exclaimed, "An excellent idea!"

"I hadn't thought of it," Ace said. "But now I will."

A photographer walked up to them. "Excuse me, guys. Could I get a picture?"

In trying to orchestrate a pose, her crutches made Nicki feel hampered. "Just a second," she said to the photog. "Here, can you hold these for just a sec?" she asked someone standing behind her.

With her booted foot bent and hidden behind her, Nicki looked as chic and fit as the rest of the group and felt happier than she had since the bike incident. Felt great when they met back up with the guys and the next day that she and Julian spent with her mother, Marie.

By Sunday the swelling in her ankle had gone down noticeably. She only took two pain pills all weekend, the second one not until just after the plane headed back west. By that night, however, she would feel another kind of pain, and her foot would have nothing to do with it.

Chapter 11

The tone of the message should have been her first clue. That her director asked her to call back no matter the time should have been the second. But when the Drake company plane touched down in Paradise Cove Sunday night, Nicki had to be awakened from a deep sleep due to the pain medication she'd taken. All she had on her mind when she pulled out her phone to take it off airplane mode was a bed and a good night's sleep.

"What's wrong?"

They'd reached Julian's car and were headed toward the townhome when she listened to the message a second time.

"Probably nothing," Nicki mumbled.

"That's not what your face says."

"Milo wants me to call him, no matter the time. Said it's urgent."

"That could be good news."

"I guess. He didn't sound too happy."

Nicki opened the browser on her phone and typed in the show's name. Familiar links she'd seen before showed up on the screen. Show's official website. Theater where the show played. Places where would-be patrons could get tickets. Nothing unusual or out of the ordinary. Then why, thought Nicki, had her heartbeat increased?

"Wonder what he wanted."

"Why don't you call and find out?"

She tapped the screen. Seven minutes past eight in California. Just after eleven on the East Coast. The show was over, Milo probably backstage. She could call and hope to get voice mail. Then again, if she didn't find out what he wanted, there'd be no sleeping tonight. That was for sure.

Her thumb hovered over the screen to hit Callback. Just before tapping the icon, she got a better idea. Swiped through to her favorites and tapped the smiling face on her screen. After the third ring, her heart fell. Paige was probably backstage, too. Or still had the phone silenced, as they all did until after leaving the theater.

"Nick! Oh my God. I was just getting ready to call you. What the hell?"

"What do you mean? What's going on?" Nicki's voice sounded as panicked as she felt. Julian looked over, immediately concerned. She put the call on speaker, getting the feeling that whatever Paige was about to say was something she'd only want to hear once.

"You don't know? Your picture is all over the internet!"

"Me? What? Where?"

"At the OTB show with the supermodel London! And her husband, Ace Montgomery!"

"And?"

"And now it looks like you're out having fun and hobnobbing with celebrities when you're under contract to work. Somebody told Milo, and he is not happy, to say the least."

Crap! How could she have been so careless? London was a celebrity. Of course the photographer would sell the pic. Caught up in the show's success and the night's excitement, she hadn't thought twice about being in the picture, had actually enjoyed being snapped as part of the group. Why shouldn't she? London was Julian's sister. And why would Milo get angry about her seeing a fashion show? Was she supposed to stay locked inside and not have any fun because she was injured? Anger replaced fear, which Nicki preferred greatly, especially since she now knew what was so urgent and why Milo had called.

"Does he know that London is my boyfriend's sister?

It's not like I was just out indiscriminately painting the town. But even if I were, wouldn't that be my business, not to mention my right? Milo knows why I'm not dancing. My foot is sprained severely, but I'm on crutches, not in a coma! Watching models walk the runway doesn't require physical labor. And there's nothing in my contract that stipulates if injured I should become a hermit until I can dance in the show again."

"No, but it's not cool to use the injury as a way to get out of doing a show to hang with your boyfriend. And that's what one of the stories implies."

Nicki couldn't talk for scrolling the screen. She'd put her name in the search bar, and all hell came up.

"Hello? Nick, you there?"

"I've got to go, Paige. Whoever said that is lying, and I've got to find out who it is."

"I knew it didn't sound like you."

"As long as I've been wanting to dance in a hit like this? And he thinks I'd skip out for any reason, especially to see a guy I've dated for years?"

"I know. It sucks."

"I've got to go."

"Okay, but call me back after talking to Milo."

Nicki ended the call while reading one of several links that mentioned her name.

They'd reached the house. Julian pulled into the garage and cut the engine. "So... Milo saw the picture we took?"

"Yes, and several more by the looks of it." She held out her phone so that Julian could see the photos. A side view as she chatted before the show. Another as she clapped and smiled. A shot of her and London hugging backstage. And the group shot, with everyone looking happy. No one looking injured. Nicki noticed not one shot included the boot on her foot or was taken as she walked on crutches. Coincidence? Sabotage? If so, by who? And why?

"There were cameras everywhere. And flashes, both from them and the lights in the show. Never thought for a second that I was the subject. There were at least a dozen photographers backstage alone. Not to mention cell phones. It could have been anyone."

"Whoever it was, the end result is the same. It's put you in a negative light. I don't like that at all."

Nicki sighed but said nothing as she continued scrolling the internet.

"Come on, babe. Let's go inside."

"Hang on. I'm looking for…"

She found the post Paige had mentioned, and the words she read cut short those she'd planned to say.

How can someone too injured to dance go to New York Fashion Week and prance? For the answer… Ask Ashley.

No question on the identity of Ashley. Next to the group shot taken on Friday night was the one from London's store, the selfie she'd taken with the woman Quinn said had a "dark heart."

Julian leaned closer. "Dang, honey. I forgot that you took a pic with that girl."

"I take selfies all the time. Quinn warned me about her, but I didn't think anything about it. I see now how that was a bad idea."

Her eyes slid from the picture back down to the text. "'Officially she has a sprained ankle. But while her cast mates were dancing it up at the Royal Theater, Nicki Long was strutting it up with celebrities…allegedly.' Not *allegedly*, you witch—"

"Babe…"

"What? She's inferring something that's totally not true."

"Exactly why you can't let her get to you, Nicki. People like her write what they hope people will read." Julian covered her hand with his and the phone along with it. "No, baby. Don't upset yourself further by reading more of that crap. You're the brightest thing shining around here, and she's just trying to catch a little light. That's all."

How could a woman stay angry with comments like that? Nicki was still beyond furious, but she appreciated what Julian was trying to do.

"You're right. They're lies. Unfortunately, some people don't know that. Like Milo. He obviously believed what he read." A sigh escaped her, as heated as the hot air Ashley blew in that article.

"I didn't know how I'd feel about being in New York and not dancing. But with you and your family, I had the best time! Was the happiest I'd been since the accident. And now this. Hurts worse than my ankle."

"We'll get it straightened out, babe. But not here. And not tonight. Let's go inside." Nicki opened her door. "Hang on. Let me help you."

Julian hopped out and came around to her side of the car.

Still holding her phone, she slipped the purse strap over her shoulder. "Where are my crutches?"

"Don't worry about that. I've got you. Put your arms around my neck."

His slender frame was misleading. But those close to him knew Julian's toned body was mostly muscle. Very little fat. Regular workouts and a decade in martial arts kept him in top form. He scooped her up effortlessly, opened the door and walked them inside.

"Thanks, babe. You can put me down now. I can make it from here."

"Without your crutches? I don't think so." Once up the stairs and inside the master suite, he walked to the bed and set her down gently. "Now…isn't that better?"

"Personal service all the way to my bed. What more can I ask for?"

"For that service to continue once you're in the bed. Glad you asked, pretty lady. Because that's exactly…" He kissed each cheek. "What…" Nuzzled her neck. "I plan to do." Slid his tongue inside her mouth. Nicki welcomed the onslaught. Julian was an excellent kisser. She'd like nothing more than to get carried away on the wings of ecstasy. But there was something she had to do.

She ended the kiss. "Let's put that on pause for when you come back up."

"What? The luggage? I can get that later." He leaned in again.

She pulled back. "I've got to call Milo. I really don't want to. Paige says he's angry. I'm not in the mood."

"Then don't call him."

"I have to. He said to call him ASAP, no matter the time."

"And you'll do that. But not tonight when you're exhausted, and reeling from someone lying about you on the internet. I think tomorrow morning is soon enough. Nine o'clock here will be noon his time."

"Thank you, Doctor. You have such a bedside manner."

"You have no idea. Just wait till I get back."

She watched him stroll out of the room. Strong, confident, saving the day. She lay back, rested against the pillow. Still very troubled about what happened, but she felt better somehow. One of the women had commented on the flight home that there was something about those Drake men. Julian's calm, steady demeanor and logical perspective was the perfect complement to her rash, more spontaneous attitude. He was right. Tomorrow would be soon enough for a conversation with the director. She'd call him on the way to get the MRI results. What more could happen between now and then to change anything?

Her cell phone pinged, indicating a text. Nicki yawned as she lifted the phone and read the screen. Vince. She sat straight up. Why was he texting? What did he want? No doubt he'd seen the stories like everyone else. She didn't want to do it but read the text anyway.

Nicki, you're balling! London's your sister? Now I know you can do a favor for a friend. Wouldn't even ask but the timing is crucial. Give me a call when you get this, ASAP.

Nicki deleted the text. Fell back on the bed. Just moments ago she'd wondered what else bad could happen. She'd just found out.

Chapter 12

Bad moods were rare for Julian. Most people dreaded Monday mornings, but they'd never been a problem for him. Whether he had a class, his internship or a patient appointment, he usually looked forward to whatever the day would bring. But there were a few things that could affect his attitude and quality of life. One of them was Nicki being unhappy. Two was not knowing exactly why. The injury was part of it, sure. But he was more focused on what had happened the previous evening. The change in Nicki's mood when he returned from the car. The mood that had shifted again this morning, as with stilted conversation she tried to cover up what bothered her.

"I appreciate you taking me back for the MRI."

"Of course. It's no problem."

With no patients scheduled on Mondays, driving her to the specialist didn't mar his day at all. There was nothing he would have handled at the office this morning that couldn't be done later at home. Being behind the wheel instead of behind a desk right now worked to his advantage. Preoccupied with the mystery going on in his home, he might not have accomplished a thing anyway.

After returning with their luggage, she hadn't wanted to make love. What could have happened to change her feelings so abruptly? Not the sudden return of pain in her ankle, as she'd claimed. Or fatigue from a pain pill when she tossed and turned half the night. There was more to it, but he hadn't pushed. Silence, Julian had learned, was a valuable tool when desiring to learn someone's true feelings. People usually shared much more information when given voluntarily without being pushed.

"I'm sorry for fading out on you last night."

"You're feeling better this morning. That's all that matters. Still no pain?"

"No, and I haven't had to take a pain pill. Makes me cautiously optimistic that I'll have good news for Milo."

"You think so?"

"Yes. Paige texted this morning and said my understudy is still being listed as a substitute and not my replacement. The grade-two sprain that was diagnosed in New York can take four to six weeks to heal. I'm hoping that my being in shape can cut off a week or two and I can be back in the show sooner rather than later."

"You don't want to risk a greater injury by going back to work prematurely."

"Wearing a protective bandage can help. And I won't start out full on—maybe eighty percent."

"I know how much you want to be back on stage, babe. Here's hoping that your dream comes true."

They reached the diagnostic center. Much like on Friday, Nicki and Julian didn't have a long wait. This time they were directed to an office instead of an examination room. Dr. Allen entered with a smile on his face. Julian hoped Nicki would leave with one on hers.

"Good morning, Nicki. Julian."

"Good morning," Julian said.

"Morning," Nicki said. "You'll tell me whether it's good or not."

"I've heard that any morning you wake up on this side of the dirt is a pretty good one." He sat behind the desk. "How was your weekend?"

The worst possible question, Julian thought, as he watched mixed emotions flit across Nicki's face.

"Long," she finally said. "My director is waiting to hear from me. I'm hoping not to be replaced."

"Then I won't keep you waiting. The bruising that garnered my concern was indicative of a more serious problem than the grade-two sprain that was initially diagnosed. You have an avulsion fracture."

Nicki's whole body slumped as she sat back against the chair. "A chipped bone?"

"A bone fragment has separated from the larger bone and the adjoining tendons. I'm sorry, Nicki. I know this isn't what you wanted to hear."

"What's the shortest amount of healing time?"

"I'd recommend no less than six weeks, especially since you were misdiagnosed and the ankle wasn't casted immediately. There's been no time for the bone fragment to reattach and set. I do believe it's close enough to that larger bone that a soft cast will stabilize it and surgery will not be required."

"A cast or surgery. Those are my options?"

"Absolutely not. You can continue to wear the boot and take your chances on whether or not the bone will heal correctly. You might even be able to do moderate dance. But maybe not. Either way you'll more than likely end up with chronic pain that can only be alleviated through surgery."

Nicki put her head in her hands. Julian reached over to comfort her. Nicki shook him off. "I'm okay." She took a deep breath and lifted her head. Her eyes looked misty, but no tears fell. "I'll do the cast."

Dr. Allen nodded. "That's a good and wise answer. The sooner you are on the road to healing, the sooner you'll be back to doing what you love."

Less than hour later, Julian helped Nicki to the car. He'd have broken his own ankle to help hers heal, but all he could do was support her as much as possible in any way that he could. They got buckled in and were soon on their way back to Paradise Cove.

"Are you hungry?" Nicki shook her head as she looked out the window. He watched her hand squeeze into a fist, knew she was resisting the urge to cry. His heart broke a little. The therapist kicked in. He remained quiet, giving her space until they merged onto the highway. It was midmorning. Traffic was light. The sun was bright. A total contrast to the gloomy, heavy atmosphere in the car.

"Baby, I'm sorry this happened to you. I can't imagine how devastating it must feel to work as hard as you have and reach your goal, only to have one of life's crazy flukes derail your plans." Julian didn't expect a response and didn't get one. "While dealing with day-to-day struggles, we often get used to hiding our feelings. We're told to be strong. Suck it up. Keep it moving, and all that. But you know I'm a safe zone, right? Where you can acknowledge the sadness, let the tears flow. It's best to get it out, babe, because otherwise those feelings will expand, deepen and cloud every thought and situation that you encounter."

She remained quiet. Julian let her be. As outgoing as she was in social situations and especially when she was on the stage, he was familiar with the side that she now revealed. Quiet. Private. Figuring it out on her own, in her head. Ironic, he thought, as Nicki reached for the cell phone in her purse. Patients paid a high fee to receive his counsel. Nicki could receive it for free, yet often kept her own.

"Might as well get this over with," Nicki mumbled.

Julian glanced over as she tapped her cell phone screen. "The call to Milo?"

"I've anticipated being fired before, but never considered having an injury cause me to leave a show. I've danced for almost fifteen years straight and never had to quit one. Why now?"

Julian remained quiet and instead heard Nicki leaving a message asking Milo to call her. After finishing the call, she adjusted her body, reclined the seat slightly and closed her eyes. Whether from exhaustion or avoidance, he didn't know. Remembering her restless night, he figured it was probably some of both.

He sympathized with Nicki, but it didn't extend to sadness. Everything happened for a reason. Julian felt this was no different. Her career was always the excuse she'd given for not moving west. For now, that barrier was gone. He hoped she'd stay in Paradise Cove during the recovery process, for the six to eight weeks Dr. Allen recommended. Perhaps in that time she'd come to love the town as he did, enough to leave New York for good. It was a selfish thought. Julian knew he should feel bad for having it. But he didn't. The only niggle that remained was from last night's situation and Nicki's mood swing. Why was he still so focused on that? Why had it bothered him so much?

More than likely it was due to the show, he decided, and the thought of having to leave it. He spent the next several miles shifting his thinking and imagining a life with Nicki in Paradise Cove. For that to happen, he'd have to get up the nerve to propose again. Nicki had no idea how she'd hurt him when she turned him down two years ago. He wanted to ask her. He wanted her to be his wife. But he didn't think his ego could survive a second no. Another rejection and their relationship would be over. And if she returned to New York? What would he do then? How long was he willing to endure a long-distance relationship and a life lived alone?

Not much longer, he realized. As they neared PC, Julian had a sobering thought. Their relationship might be ending right now.

Chapter 13

Nicki looked at her phone for the tenth time in five minutes, then placed it on the kitchen island, determined to walk away and leave it there. It was the only way she'd stop checking the ringer volume or text messages to ensure she hadn't missed a message or call from Milo, returning her call from yesterday.

She reached for the crutches leaning against the granite countertop and headed out of the room as fast she could hop. It was hard to run away from one's thoughts on crutches. As she passed the dining space into the living room they followed her. So what if it had been almost twenty-four hours since she'd left Milo a message. There were any number of reasons why he hadn't returned her call. It could have nothing to do with the fashion show pictures and the past weekend's gossip. Milo would never doubt her passion for dancing, uncompromising work ethic or belief in the show. Until the accident she'd never missed rehearsal. Never been late. More often than not, she'd been one of the first ones there and one of the last to go home. She'd worked herself ragged to get a difficult sequence perfected, the timing just right. Milo knew about her dreams of Broadway, had said she was one of the hungriest performers he'd ever seen.

As for not calling on Friday? That was no big deal, either. The reason was simple. She hadn't any news until yesterday—which was the worst news possible, with dire consequences. But a short time after receiving the cast and leaving the hospital, she'd put on her big-girl panties and called the director. He needed to call her back. ASAP. The waiting hurt worse than her ankle ever did.

Reaching the expansive glass doors, she slid one of them open and walked out into the crisp morning air. The coming of autumn had not only brought cooler temps, but colorful foliage on the red maple and sweetgum trees planted in the backyard. Nicki noticed how the leaves' colors complemented the patio's natural stone tile, highlighted the red and orange shards amid the tan and gray. They reminded her of the trees in Prospect Park near her childhood home. She used to collect them as she played on Saturday mornings and take them to school for Monday's show and tell.

Time to go back, she thought as she watched a bird sail over the fence and perch on one of the higher branches. She didn't want to be a burden to Julian, or draw his family's pity. Even with crutches she could navigate Brooklyn. She had more resources there—she knew her neighbors. Could grab a bus, train or taxi down the street from her house. Maybe Julian could come for a visit in November, celebrate Thanksgiving in New York. Almost eight weeks away. A long time to be without her man. The only thing good about the thought was that by then she'd be back dancing.

She reached a patio chair and leaned her crutch against the table. Just as she was about to sit down, her phone rang. "Just like a watched pot," she mumbled, grabbing the crutch and hightailing it back to the kitchen as fast as she could.

"Hello?"

"Hey, superstar."

Crap! Vince. Too late, she glanced at the screen. Wouldn't have helped. The call hadn't come in as private but with a number she didn't recognize but probably would have answered since it began with a Brooklyn area code: 929.

"What, you don't have any conversation for an old friend?"

"No, Vince. We've already had what should have been our last conversation two conversations ago."

"You didn't get my text?"

"I got it but I didn't understand it. Taking a picture with a group of celebrities doesn't put money in my bank account."

"Not just celebrities. Your sister."

"London isn't my sister."

"Your boyfriend's sister. Same thing."

"Who have you been talking to?"

"The internet. Info at your fingertips, girl. No secrets anymore."

Nicki wished she'd remembered that after giving Vince her number. Had she done so she would have realized two very important words he'd left out of the description "pro basketball player"—*former* and *broke*.

"Who I'm dating and his family tree have nothing to do with what you asked me months ago. I didn't have money to loan you then and I still don't."

"Ask your man for the money. He should be able to take care of you at least as good as I did."

The comment was audacious and wrong and rolled off his tongue much too glibly. As though it wasn't being said for the first time. So quickly did she want to rebut the lie, Nicki almost bit her tongue. "Oh, so that's how you've re-written our very brief history together. I wondered how you could possibly come to someone you barely knew a month and ask for that much money. It's because you've fabricated an experience that didn't happen. I've taken care of myself since I was seventeen years old and worked hard for every dime I've earned. Just like I worked for and won the audition in Atlanta. The director exposed your lie two years ago. I didn't owe you then, and get this straight—I don't owe you now."

Vince laughed as though she'd just told a joke. Nicki wasn't laughing at all.

"Your attitude doesn't surprise me. Nor does your gall.

Next time it won't be me saying this. It will be my attorney or a judge. Lose my number."

"I'm not playing with you, Nicki. I borrowed money from the wrong people. Now I owe them. And you owe me. I intend to collect. Don't make me—"

She ended the call and seconds later heard the garage door opening. Unexpected since Julian usually called before coming home to see what she needed or suggest eating out. Earlier than he usually broke for lunch, too. Had something happened? Was he okay? And what if Vince decided to call again? That's exactly what he did. She refused the call and muted her phone just as Julian walked into the kitchen.

"Hi."

The barest of pauses between strides. "Hey, babe." He walked over. Hugged her. "Your heart's racing. I excite you like that?" His eyes were intent, but he smiled.

"Of course." She playfully pushed past him and put the wide granite island between them. "But I'm on edge, too."

"The director called?"

"No."

"That's got you nervous." Nicki didn't answer, just kind of half shrugged. "Totally understandable that it would. Think you should call again?"

"I don't want to appear as anxious as I feel. Wasn't expecting you, either, so hearing the garage door startled me."

"It was a spontaneous decision. A nice day, and I felt like getting out of the office. But perhaps I should have called."

"I'm glad you're here. Crutches are helpful, but I like you carrying me much better." One second she was standing, the next her feet had left the floor. Nicki let out a sound of surprise.

Julian had picked her up as though she weighed nothing, carried her across the room and set her down on the couch.

He flopped down beside her. "Better?"

"Actually, yes. Thank you."

"With nervousness probably putting your stomach in knots, is it safe for me to assume that you haven't eaten?"

"I had a protein shake earlier. Does that count?"

"Like I figured." Julian eased off the couch. "I'm going to run down to the deli. They've got great soups, sandwiches and salads. Going to bring you back something and you're going to eat it. Okay?"

"Sure." Julian walked away, but when Nicki's phone buzzed he came back into the living room. His eyes asked a question. In answer, Nicki held up her cell phone, which showed the face of a smiling man with curly black hair and a bright feather earring in his right ear. Milo.

Nicki answered the call and put it on speaker. "Milo?" She watched Julian sit on the short side of the L-shaped sectional with her directly in his line of sight.

"Hello, Nicki. How are you?"

"I've been better."

"From what I hear, things are fine."

Nicki looked at Julian. She was almost sure what Milo was talking about but refused to be the one to mention the pictures from fashion week.

"What did you hear?"

"That you were in New York last week. Partying it up at the OTB show. Can't dance on that ankle, but it appears you can walk just fine. You should have stopped by."

"Watch the show I'm supposed to be in, with someone else dancing my part? I can't believe you'd suggest that, Milo. Sitting this show out is the hardest thing I've ever done. Yes, I was in New York. London is my boyfriend's sister. They thought going to the show would cheer me up. But I was and still am very much on crutches, with an injury that's even worse than I thought. So please don't believe everything you read, Milo. This is hard enough."

"Perception is reality, Nicki. Especially in this town. You were supposed to call on Friday. You didn't. Then you're snapped at fashion week, leaving me to have to explain to investors why you were too injured to work but not too hurt to party. That was pretty difficult, too."

"I'm sorry, Milo. You're right. I should have called. I didn't because there was no new information. The doctor wanted to do an MRI before making an official diagnosis. We just got the results yesterday. I called right after."

"What's the verdict?"

"Chipped bone. Soft cast. Out for at least four more weeks."

"Ouch."

"Exactly."

"I'm sorry, Nicki."

"Me, too. I know that's a long time, but I'm hoping there's a way you can save my spot and let me come back. I've worked so hard—"

"You know I can't do that. This is a short run, only sixteen weeks. In three weeks Arielle will have been in the role longer than you. The audience loves her. So do the investors. It's rotten timing. Lousy luck. But there's no way I can guarantee you that spot."

"But the investors love you too, Milo. And you know how dedicated I am to this show! If you tell them you want me in that role, they'll listen. Maybe it won't take six weeks. If it guarantees that I won't lose the role, I can work my ass off and be back in four."

"It's too late, Nicki. Asking you to call on Friday wasn't just to inquire about your health. It was to inform you that while you were great, and you know how much I love how you dance, the investors prefer Arielle. Especially the one based in LA who wants to transition the show from Broadway to the big screen. She's pulled for her from the very beginning. Thinks the camera will love her. Arielle will take over the part permanently, beginning this week."

Milo kept talking, but Nicki didn't hear much more after that. The call ended. She was vaguely aware of Julian coming to sit next to her, his arms going around her. A river of tears came up from her belly. She batted her eyelids and swallowed the pain. The tears lodged in her throat. She wouldn't cry. What good would it do? It was time to go home. The faster she went back, the faster she and her agent could start working on the next gig. Finding upcoming shows. Taking meetings and networking. She would not let a chipped bone chip away her dream of Broadway and stardom. She was too close to stop now.

Julian kissed her temple. Nicki grabbed her throat lest the cry escape.

"What are you thinking, baby?"

"Calling my agent," she replied, her voice raspy with pent-up emotion. She cleared her throat. "Setting up meetings. And making a reservation to fly back home."

Nicki knew it wasn't the answer he wanted to hear. She didn't want to leave, either. Mostly because of how much she loved Julian, but there was another reason. Vince was in New York, along with the thugs, the threats and the fear that one of their angry taunts would be carried out.

Chapter 14

The next morning Julian arrived at the office with what he thought were big problems. By the afternoon his perspective had changed. His first appointment was slowly rebuilding her life after relocating to PC following the unspeakable trauma of discovering a teenage son who'd committed suicide. The second appointment battled guilt over surviving an accident where his best friend was killed. It had happened years ago, but the pain was as fresh as if it had happened yesterday.

Julian released his last patient with a referral to a psychiatrist. There were times when medication was mandatory and the war vet's severe PTSD and dysthymia presented one of those times. He'd gone out for lunch, walked around the square to clear his head. He sat and thought about the dilemmas that hours ago had felt enormous. Nicki leaving was no small matter, and the increasing number of patients wanting to switch from Dr. Johnson's care to his was disconcerting at best. But in comparison to what some people in the world had to deal with, Julian counted himself a lucky man.

The sound of a cell phone broke into his thoughts. A programmed series of chimes informed Julian that it was the call he'd expected. He retrieved the phone from where it sat on the desk and walked back to the window.

"Hello, Mom."

"Good afternoon, son. How are you?"

"I'm good."

"Julian, I've known you since the day you were born. You're handling business effectively as always, but what's been said about Nicki has got to upset you. How could it not?"

With what had happened since then and his shift in perspective, he'd almost forgotten about Ashley's blog. "I'm not happy about what was written. But there are way worse problems than gossip, Mom."

"What do you mean?"

Suicide. War. Chronic depression. "Nicki's out of the show."

"Oh no! What happened?"

He told her. "Ashley's post was untimely and in poor taste," he finished. "But it was the chipped bone that got her released."

"Nicki must be devastated."

"It was her worst-case scenario."

"That still doesn't excuse what Ashley's done and continues to do. Did you know she talked to *XYZ*?"

"I did not." Nor did he care, at the moment.

"We should have handled that Ashley matter years ago after what happened with Niko. But your father talked me out of it. Felt as you did, that she and her mother were minor, insignificant and should be ignored. Now your lady has become fodder for tabloid media, and that conniver who's been trying to come up for years sees another bootstrap to try and ride up on since she can't seem to use her own. Well, I know you are not going to stand for that, and the members of your family, darling, stand with you."

"Mom, you know I'm not good at this kind of stuff. I don't fight with people like her. I treat them."

"I treat them, too, dear. We only differ on the prescription."

"Besides, Ashley isn't the one behind that smear campaign. Someone angry at me used her as a pawn."

"Go on."

"No need. I'll handle it."

"Of course you will. You always do. You're the only child of mine who can do so without my having one inkling about what's going on. It's something that I find equally admirable and annoying." Julian truly laughed for the first time all day. "What will Nicki do now?"

"Go back to New York. Start looking for work."

"But you just said she's out for at least six weeks. Why does she feel the need to go back so quickly?"

"It's home. She feels more comfortable there. Able to do things, move around, with a support system of her neighbors and friends, and her mother in New Jersey."

"Does she know about her support system in Paradise Cove? What happens to one of us happens to all of us. Tell her that. Never mind, I will. Please remind her of the lunch date we discussed over the weekend. Let her know I'll be calling tomorrow to firm up those plans."

Julian knew Jennifer. There was a motive for this meal. "I'll let her know."

"Good. I'm excited to share an idea with her."

"As long as whatever you have in mind can happen from New York. She's planning to leave at the end of the week. I doubt those plans will change."

"Is that what you want?"

Julian thought about what he'd wanted, and what had happened that night in Times Square when he'd worked up the nerve to act on his desire. Hadn't turned out so good.

"Julian, did you hear me?"

"I heard you. I want Nicki to be where she's happy. At the end of the...hold on, Mom." He muted his cell phone and pushed the intercom button. "Yes, Katie?"

"You have a visitor, Dr. Drake."

Julian slowly stood, his voice calm. "Who is it?" Natalie? At the mere thought his back stiffened, despite his resolve not to react. He was so not in the mood.

"It's your brother."

His body relaxed. "Which one?"

The door opened. Ike walked in. "Your eldest brother, Doctor. The one who matters most."

Julian unmuted his cell phone. The unexpected interruption brought out a smile. "Mom, I have a visitor. Let's talk later."

"Sure, son. Love you. Goodbye."

Julian motioned for Ike to have a seat, then sat behind the desk. Ike bypassed the two modern chairs facing Julian's desk and walked into the seating area where he saw patients. There was a fabric-covered love seat done in a geometric charcoal and gray print with blue microdots breaking the monotony. A similar chair to those facing Julian's desk was by the love seat, in the same color blue as the dots on the couch. On the opposite wall was a leather chaise. Across the back was a colorful fleece throw for those patients who felt more comfortable lying down when baring their souls and their problems.

Ike nodded his approval as he returned to the desk. "Very nice, little brother." He sat, continued to look around with an expression of wonder mixed with pride. "These offices have the look and feel of a bona fide psychologist."

"Imagine that."

"Not cold and impersonal, though, like those stereotypical ones you see in the movies. It feels comfortable, warm. Mom handled the interior decorating, I assume?"

"It's signature Jennifer."

"I've often said the only difference between Mom and the people she hires is their degree." Ike looked at Julian. "I'm proud of you, man. Still remember you at family gatherings off in some corner with a computer or book. So quiet. Missing nothing. I should have known you'd grow into someone focused on the mind."

"You clearly had heading up the family business on lock, so I had to find my lane."

"Ah, so that's how it happened?" Ike stretched out his legs, clasped his hands behind his head. "You were never all that into the business, though you would have made an excellent CFO. Sales? Not so much. On account of to sell a property you have to talk and all."

"Which is why Terrell as sales VP is a perfect fit." Said with that almost smile. He looked at his watch. "So, Ike, to what do I owe this pleasure? Since it hasn't happened before, I appreciate you coming by the office, but I doubt it was just to check out the decor."

"That was part of it. A visit to see the end result of a decade in college was long overdue."

"And the other part?"

"I wanted to see how you were holding up, not how you said you were doing, because that answer is always 'good' or 'fine.' But you're the quiet one. You don't do drama. So I came to see for myself how this weekend's scandal has affected you."

"I learned how not to do drama by watching you. Terrell is who I expected to come by."

"Come by to add to it?"

Julian nodded with gleeful eyes. "But then again, guess life has never been the same for you since Quinn shook you up."

"Are you equating my wife with drama?" Ike asked in a way that suggested Julian should be careful of his answer.

"Absolutely," Julian replied, totally carefree.

"You'd be right. I know you know, but I wanted to tell you personally that anything we can do to help, anything you or Nicki need, just let us know. Maybe you guys can come over Friday night. Quinn would love that. She once dreamed of being a ballerina. I think she's a little starstruck."

"She's flying home on Friday."

"How'd you run her away, bro?"

"She misses New York."

The intercom beeped. "Excuse me, Dr. Drake?"

"Yes."

"Could you pick up, please?"

Julian knew the call was about a patient, and Katie was following protocol to maintain privacy. "Okay."

"It's Frank Snyder calling. Again."

"Take a message. And can you pull his file and draft a formal letter with my explicit instructions for him to continue seeing his present psychiatrist?"

"Sure, Doctor."

"And please do the same for the folders placed in your inbox. There should be three or four. Thanks."

He replaced the receiver, brow furrowed.

"Problem?"

"A situation." Julian leaned against the chair back, idly rubbing his chin as he pondered the call. "Several of Dr. Johnson's patients wanting my help."

"Current patients?"

Julian nodded.

"Why?"

"Speaking generally, there are many reasons why it happens. Feeling uncomfortable, not with the treatment but with the person. Not connecting. No rapport. Or too comfortable, not feeling challenged, not progressing at the rate or level one thinks they should. Trust is paramount to healing, and what establishes that trust is subjective. Not long ago an associate of mine lost a client because he's a Mets fan and the patient was a Yankees season ticket holder."

Ike shrugged. "It's a free country. If people want to change therapists and come to you, it's their choice, right?"

"Yes."

"Why is that a problem?"

"Because in a town this size, Johnson knows what's happening."

"Did he confront you?"

"He didn't have to. Natalie did."

"I don't know her."

"We went to grade and middle school together."

"Look, don't give the competition another thought."

"I'm not competing with anyone."

"When there's a shared goal, a choice to be made and money involved, it's competition. This isn't personal, it's business. Sounds like Dr. Johnson might have a problem. Because when it comes to competition, Drakes always win."

"Thanks, Ike." Julian stood. "I'm glad you stopped by."

Ike stood as well. "I've overstayed my welcome so you're kicking me out?"

"No, I'm escorting you out. Duty calls."

Julian returned to his desk, glad his brother had decided to stop by. Ike had lifted his spirits and given him resolve. His brother was right. Drakes didn't lose. When it came to wanting something, they went all out to get it. And Julian wanted Nicki to stay in PC.

He looked at his watch. Five minutes until his client arrived. He turned to his laptop, checked his schedule, made some changes and then clicked on a search engine. Nicki might go home on Friday. But it wouldn't be for his lack of trying to convince her otherwise.

Chapter 15

Vince hadn't followed Nicki's suggestion to lose her number. Instead he'd texted or called almost a dozen times since yesterday. That she knew of—could have been more. He'd only left one voice mail, ratcheting up the danger he faced. Demanding she call him. But there'd been a few calls from unknown numbers, too. She hadn't answered, and no messages had been left from those numbers. Even if she'd had an inkling to, which she hadn't, what was revealed in the texts wouldn't have changed her mind.

Nicki reached for her tablet and clicked on the app she'd downloaded that morning—a way to save the text messages in a printable document, a backup in case they disappeared from her phone. She typed in her password. The app opened up to Vince's messages. Exchanges that had changed in topic and tone. Growing more erratic. More threatening. More desperate. Making Nicki more uneasy with each note she read.

The phone on the counter vibrated. Nicki jumped, startled. She chanced a glance, hoping that instead of the 929 prefix of Vince's number, she'd see the friendly face of a number she'd saved. A wide, impish smile and bright green eyes looked back at her.

"Paige! I'm so glad it's you."

"I'm glad you answered. You didn't last night."

"I'd silenced the phone. Checked messages this morning, though, and didn't get yours."

"Didn't leave one. Figured you'd call back when you saw the missed call."

"I've been trying not to look at my phone."

"Oh no! Is it the reporters? Are you being hounded about

the fashion show pics or this morning's press release? I'm so sorry for you, Nicki. It just isn't fair."

"That I've been released from the show? They announced it?"

"Sounds like you knew already."

"Milo called me yesterday."

"What did he say? Because I thought he'd agreed to hold your spot for the four weeks it would take to heal."

"Looks like it's going to take longer than that. Besides, the investors like what Arielle brings to the role. They're considering a film version of the show and want her in it."

"How do they figure when you are clearly the better dancer? What she brings to the role? What does that mean?"

"Doesn't matter. Like I said, the injury is worse than first diagnosed. It'll take six to eight weeks to heal. She would have replaced me anyway."

"Your ankle is broken?"

"Fractured. The doctor in New York didn't see the full extent of the injury. The specialist Julian's family recommended, a doctor who specializes in sports injuries, was concerned about the bruising still visible after two weeks. He did an MRI and discovered that a piece of bone had been chipped off."

"Yikes!"

"Yep. And that I've tried to put pressure on it didn't help. Now I'm in a cast for the next two weeks to keep the ankle immobile so the bone can reattach. Where'd you read the announcement about the change?"

"The cast got an email last night."

"It's probably everywhere by now."

"This is such a bummer, Nicki. What are you going to do?"

"Paige, to be honest, I don't know. With everything going on, it may be a blessing in disguise."

"How so?"

"Vince is still contacting me, to the point where I'm getting a little freaked out."

"What is he saying?"

"He only left one voice mail, demanding I call him. But he's left these texts." Nicki tapped on the messages icon. "The first one said, 'You hanging up on me now? This is not a game!' I didn't respond. The second one. 'Come on, Nicki, I need this. These guys want their money now!' The third one. 'They'll back off if I send at least half. Can you loan me ten K? Today? Use PayPerson with this number.' The fourth one. 'I'm going to get my money one way or the other.'"

"Oh my gosh, Nick! That's an all-out threat!"

"Yep, and it's this last one that really got me. It says, 'Those guys think you're the problem. Do they need to pay you another visit?'"

"Okay, that's it. He's taken this to a whole other level. When are you coming back? As soon as you do, you need to go to the police, tell them everything and get a restraining order."

"Agreed. But will that be enough?"

"What else can you do?"

Nicki saw that a new message had come in. She tapped her screen to open it and read the text from Julian. "Right now I'm going to get off the phone and get dressed to go out. Julian just texted me saying he'd be by in an hour and be ready to go."

"Have you told him yet?"

"No, and I have my reasons so don't go there. I already know how you feel."

"You need to tell him, Nicki. Not necessarily about the affair, but definitely about the threats. Promise me you will."

"I never thought about revealing the threats but not the affair. But you're right. There's no need for him to know that part of the story. You have my word, Paige. I'll tell him today."

A short time later, Julian breezed into the house with the signature subconscious swagger of a confident Drake. He'd gone from feeling sad about Nicki's inevitable leaving to being excited about the challenge of trying to convince her to stay.

"Nicki!"

"Yeah, babe. Up here!"

"You ready?" He took the steps quickly to see for himself.

"Just about."

He entered the master suite. "Where are you?"

"In here." Nicki turned while putting on an earring as he reached the en suite doorway and leaned against the jamb.

"I thought I told you to be ready, woman!"

"I am."

"Ready would have been downstairs on the couch waiting with purse in hand."

"Where are we going? Is this okay?"

Julian took in her outfit, brown velvet palazzo pants, matching cropped turtleneck, a tan leather ankle boot on one foot and a knitted bootie over her cast. Several strands of vibrantly colored wooden beads completed the fall look.

"It's perfect." He stepped in and gave her a kiss. "Let's go," he said, glancing at his watch as he reached for her hand. "Our plane is scheduled for takeoff in thirty minutes."

Nicki snatched back her hand and reached for the second wooden hoop lying on the counter. "Plane? Where are we going? And why didn't you tell me to pack?"

"Someplace special. Come on. We need to leave."

"Julian!" She reached for the crutch leaning against the wall. "Move! I need to throw a few—"

He grabbed her hand once again and halted her progress. "You don't need to do anything but grab your purse and maybe your makeup. I'll take care of whatever else you need."

"Take care of me having something to wear? How, by buying me a whole new wardrobe?"

"If that's what it takes to get you out of this bathroom and into the car. Now, are you going to use that crutch or should I carry you down? Never mind." He scooped her up and headed toward the door.

"Wait, Julian. My purse!"

"I'll come back for it."

"Don't make picking me up a habit. I can walk on my own."

"Why? I thought women liked being swept off their feet."

Minutes later the couple were off and headed for the landing strip that serviced private planes.

"Where are we going?"

Julian glanced over, turned on the car's music system, kept on driving. Nicki huffed and crossed her arms.

"Baby, listen." He gave her a sexy look. "Remember this?" He turned up the volume. "I'm addicted, and I just can't get enough."

Nicki pouted, gave him a side eye.

"Come on, babe. That crazy party you invited me to. What was that, our second date or third one?"

Nicki's pout deepened. "I don't remember."

Julian laughed out loud. A rare sound. "Yes, you do!" He bobbed his head to the beat. "Come on, you know you want to dance. This is one of your favorite groups. Then there's this one."

Bruno Mars's lilting voice oozed out of the speakers and made Nicki smile.

"You remember what happened after we heard this?"

"No."

"Liar!" Julian laughed again as he turned up the volume.

"Of course I remember," Nicki said after a time. "That was the night we first made love."

The night she found out twenty-one-year-old Julian was a virgin, and learned the conservative view he held when it came to sex. Not the act. Julian was a freak between the sheets. But that lovemaking was special, not something to be done with just anyone. "What's with this trip down memory lane? You trying to tell me something?"

"Absolutely."

"What?"

Julian pulled into the parking lot next to the hangar where private planes were stored when not in use. Looked into Nicki's anxious eyes.

"That we're getting ready to make more memories, even more beautiful than the ones we made that night."

Chapter 16

Though Julian offered both a wheelchair and his arms as transporting devices, Nicki insisted on getting through the hangar to the landing strip on her own strength. It should have been a given since they hadn't driven to a commercial airport, but Nicki didn't realize they were taking a private plane until she saw the same sleek aircraft they'd boarded to New York a week ago. Even so, she asked the obvious.

"We're taking the company plane?"

"We are indeed."

"I thought you said it was only used for business."

"This is somewhat of a business trip."

"How so?"

"It will become clearer as the evening unfolds. Can you make it up the stairs or should I inform the attendant to convert it to a ramp so that you can use the wheelchair?"

"I can make it." Julian reached up and placed a hand at her elbow, a move that got him reprimanded. "I've got it, Julian. Just give me a second."

"I'm just offering support, Nicki. The last thing we want is for you to have a mishap that results in another injury."

Nicki reached the top of the stairs, quietly greeted the cautious attendant and sat down in the first available seat. She watched Julian enter behind her. He chatted casually with the attendant before the pilot joined them. The three laughed at something before the pilot shook Julian's hand and walked into the cockpit.

Nicki watched how comfortable Julian was in these luxurious surroundings, as if flying in this manner was normal. She wondered what it was like to have grown up in wealth and privilege. Nicki's mom had done an excellent job in providing for her only child. Nicki's father had died when she was young, tragically killed in a freak motorcycle accident. Nicki hadn't lived in excess by any means. Her mother hadn't spoiled her. She'd been given everything she needed and quite a few things that she wanted as well. Yet in the last few minutes, she realized, it was him who'd acted like one with stellar home training and her who'd played the spoiled brat. Julian was only trying to be helpful, obviously taking her on this trip to feel better about losing her Broadway job. She should be thanking him for being so generous. Instead she was acting like a witch.

He slowly approached her. "Is it safe for me to sit beside you or should I find my own row?"

"I'm sorry for snapping at you." Nicki patted the seat beside her. "Sit down. Please."

He reached for her hand, held it as he spoke but did not look at her. "I can understand you being upset. I know how much your career means to you. But I get the feeling that something else is going on, Nicki." He looked at her then. "What is it?"

"You're right. There is something else."

The attendant walked up. "We'll be taking off shortly. Can I get you something to drink?"

"We're fine, thanks." Julian spoke for both them.

"Actually," Nicki said, "do you have Patrón?"

"Yes, we do."

"Could I get a margarita?"

"Salt on the rim?"

"Um, no, thank you."

"Coming right up."

She felt Julian's eyes on her. "You all right?" She nodded. "You rarely ever drink."

"I know."

"You shouldn't mix alcohol with those meds."

"I didn't take one today."

"But you're not hurting?"

Not in my ankle. "No, I'm good."

They felt the plane begin to taxi. Julian buckled his seat belt. Nicki did, too.

The attendant brought back the margarita and handed it to Nicki. "I brought you a sparkling water, Dr. Drake. I hope you don't mind."

Julian lifted the glass slightly. "Good choice. Thanks."

Nicki looked out the window. Her stomach roiled with nerves. There was simply no good time to share bad news, no pretty way to dress up ugly. With steely resolve and another sip of the tasty margarita, she began speaking.

"There is someone trying to force me to repay money I don't owe." In the ensuing silence, Nicki imagined Julian's sharp mind rapidly turning. Processing what she'd said, adding in what she hadn't. "He needs money quick and—"

"He?"

"Yes."

"He who?"

"A guy I met a couple years ago. One of his cousins directed a show I did in Atlanta. He tried to say his connection is how I got the role. It isn't. I auditioned like everyone else. But he's using the claim to try to get money. I think he borrowed from a loan shark or someone shady who's pressing pretty hard to get their money back."

Julian's eyes narrowed as he pondered what Nicki said. He took a sip of water, then another, before turning to eye her closely. "That sounds weird, like there's more to the story."

"There's a little more to it. I went out with him a couple years ago. Right after we broke up. Met him at a party, felt lonely, gave him my number. We only went out a few times. When you and I got back together, I had already blocked his number."

"That was it?"

"Pretty much. He was a jerk, obviously. I wouldn't have continued with him no matter what."

"So with his number blocked, how'd he contact you? Did he come to the show?" He turned more fully. "Is that what happened the night I was there? On opening night, when you ran to the car as though someone was chasing you?"

Nicki looked out the window. The attendant started toward them but was halted by Julian's hand.

"He was there. Waiting on the sidewalk. Didn't approach me when he saw you. But he'd called me a couple weeks before, when I answered an unknown number thinking it was someone calling about the show. It was him. He'd seen the news that I'd gotten a role on Broadway. Guess he figured, like many others, that anyone on Broadway is making tons of money. I honestly thought it was a joke, until he started talking about the show in Atlanta and how he'd talked to the director and that's how I got hired. I told him I didn't have it and even if I did, I wouldn't loan him that kind of money."

"How much does he want?"

"Twenty thousand."

"He thinks you owe him twenty thousand dollars?"

"I don't owe him anything. Twenty thousand is how much he needs. He has a gambling habit. That's one of the things I found out just before you and I got back together. He's got to be desperate to come to me, someone he dated for a month two years ago. Anyway, the harassing phone calls have continued, and gotten worse in the last few days."

"So this has been going on since the show opened." Nicki nodded. "I hate that you've dealt with this alone all this time. It's disappointing that you wouldn't reach out."

"I should have, Julian. I realize that now. But I was embarrassed to even have gone out with someone like him. Honestly, I never thought it would go this far."

"Just how far has it gone?"

Nicki hesitated. Should she tell him about the guys at her place? No, he'd definitely not want her to return home. "Threatening phone calls that I've recorded to turn over to the police. Coming to the show, but only that one time. Once I'm back in New York, I'll get a restraining order. I think that will put an end to it. I don't think he wants to go to jail."

"I think you should consider staying here with me."

"I knew you'd say that."

"Why not? At least for now. You can't dance or even try out for six to eight weeks."

"But I can meet with my agent, check out what's available and be there if a director wants to meet."

"You can do all of that from here and handle the initial meeting over the phone."

"I just want to get back, that's all. But I'll think about it. Okay?"

"Okay."

"Still won't tell me where we're going?"

"You'll know when we get there. When is the last time you heard from this guy?"

"A couple days ago. I told him the conversation was being recorded and that I was going to the police. I don't think he'll call again."

"Let me know if he does."

"Okay."

"I mean it, Nicki. I'm all too familiar with your independent streak. But don't keep me out of the loop on this. I can't take care of you if I don't know what's going on."

"Okay, I will." Nicki leaned over, kissed his cheek and

then nestled against him. "I feel better having told you." He nodded, kissed her temple. "Know something else?"

"Hmm."

"It's probably good I'm not a drinker. That tequila makes me horny."

"In that case… Kim! Can we get another margarita, please?"

"Don't, Kim!" Nicki gave Julian's arm a playful swat. "But I'd love some sparkling water."

"Sure, coming right up."

A comfortable silence fell between them as Kim brought out Nicki's drink and a tray of hot appetizers. Nicki looked out the window. Before dating Julian, she'd never been west. Was still struck at the stark difference between the East and West Coast topographies. Back east there'd be shades of green from various trees, even oranges, reds and tans from leaves changing color. The view of the west from the sky was filled with reds and browns, vast, seemingly uninhabited tracts of earth punctuated by cities that cropped up here and there. Like the one that seemed to be coming into view. Not Oakland, as she'd imagined, and another visit to the Drake condo in San Francisco. No, this city was bigger. And what was that layer of brown hovering several feet below the crowds? Was it…

"Los Angeles! You're taking me to LA?"

"Can't keep a secret from you forever, huh?"

"I've never been to Los Angeles and always wanted to go."

"We'll be there in about—" Julian checked his watch "—fifteen minutes."

"This was a perfect answer for my doldrums. Thank you, Julian. Really. I love you so much."

"You're welcome, baby."

The plane began its descent. Nicki craned her neck to

take in the vast metropolis known as the City of Angels. Hard to believe, but in the moment she actually felt happy. Something she'd thought impossible just hours ago. Paige was right. Julian should know what was going on. Nicki felt better that she'd told him and hoped what she said was true—that Vince would heed her warning and stop the threatening phone calls and texts. If he scared her like this while she was out on the West Coast, who knew what could happen back east.

Chapter 17

There was so much to see! Julian had the driver take the streets instead of the highway so that Nicki could appreciate all the diverse and plentiful neighborhoods that made up metropolitan LA. Thirty minutes into their ride, they'd already passed more than half a dozen: Ladera Heights, Inglewood, Baldwin Hills and View Park. A native Angeleno, the driver gave exciting history about the famous Crenshaw Boulevard that ran from Wilshire Boulevard all the way into Long Beach and was once the cruising route for lowriders and hydraulic wonders, a street that rappers immortalized in catchy tunes. Who knew about Leimert Park's rich history, where so many famous comedians honed their craft? Past West Adams and mid-Wilshire, they headed east through Koreatown and into downtown.

"What do you think?" Julian smiled broadly. Clearly, he enjoyed watching Nicki's virginal journey through the concrete jungles of the country's second-largest city.

"Everything's so spread out. Looks different than I expected. Don't know what that was, but…"

"Probably what you've seen on TV. Beverly Hills. Hollywood. We'll see that, too. Tomorrow."

The driver turned onto a street lined with shops. Nicki turned to Julian. "Is this the garment district?"

"How'd you know?"

"Worked with a girl from LA once who told me about it. Said you could get great bargains down here, designer clothing at wholesale prices. Looks like everything's closed, though."

"It is," the driver interrupted. "Merchants pretty much close up when the business workday is over. Very few customers after around four o'clock. These streets change late at night. Not the safest place if most of your business is in cash."

Nicki turned to Julian. "Will we be able to come back tomorrow?"

"If you'd like. Though I think we might be able to get what you need tonight."

"How do you figure?"

Julian winked. "I know people."

The driver pulled over near the end of a street.

"This is it?" Julian asked.

The driver pointed at a brick building on the corner. "Right over there."

"Come on, babe. Here, let me help you." Julian reached for one of the aluminum crutches, unfolded it and then went over to Nicki's side and helped her out.

"Where are we going?"

"So many questions!"

"Because I'm not getting answers!"

They reached the door on the corner. Julian rang a doorbell. The door opened quickly. A perky blonde twentysomething stepped back as they entered. "Dr. Drake! Hello. You must be Nicki. Welcome to OTB's LA warehouse."

Nicki gasped. "OTB Her?" The warehouse assistant nodded and laughed at Nicki's obvious surprise. Nicki looked at Julian. "I can get an outfit here?"

"You're going to get several, but the clock is ticking and we've got a full agenda."

"I've already chosen some outfits I think you'll like, so if you come on back to the showroom and have a seat, I'll bring them right out."

An hour later Nicki and Julian reentered the limo, the trunk packed with originals from Julian's sister London's husband, model-turned-fashion-designer Ace Montgomery.

Nicki's eyes shone like a kid at the circus. "That was so amazing, Julian! Thank you so much."

"You're welcome, baby. It's good to see you smile."

"Where are we going tonight? Hopefully someplace I can wear that jumpsuit."

"That was my second favorite after the mini. Your ankle might be injured, but your ass has never looked better."

"Obviously, since you couldn't keep your hands off it back there while I changed."

"Wait till later tonight and see what my hands do," he said while trying to ease said hand under her top.

She smacked it away. "Behave! Where are we going?"

"To the hotel to shower and change, and then to dinner and…your next surprise."

"Another surprise? Something more than getting OTB originals? I could die right now and be a happy woman."

"Don't do that, babe. If you miss out on what's happening next, you'll really be mad."

She really would have, too. After a short ride from the OTB LA warehouse, Nicki and Julian checked into a Ritz-Carlton suite, enjoyed sushi and seafood at a five-star restaurant, and then headed to the Ahmanson Theater.

"LuLu?" Nicki read the program Julian received from one usher while another escorted them to their orchestra seats. Once settled into their seats, she read about the innovative dance troupe out of Britain, creating a buzz in LA sure to sweep the nation with a fun, fast, fiery musical that absolutely embodied the title, *lu*, the Yoruba word for "beat."

Nicki watched, transfixed, as the lead character mixed an intricate dance style with beats created by everything from percussion instruments to hands and feet, taking the audience on a journey of the heart. By intermission she'd fallen in love with the show and especially the intricate type of dance. By the time the performance ended, she wanted to be on stage dancing with them.

Julian pulled strings and got them backstage. Nicki met the director, a humble British talent who was also the show's choreographer and playwright.

"The show is fantastic!"

The director acknowledged the compliment with a slight bow. "Thank you so much."

"What type of dancing was that?"

"It's lulu dancing, moving to and with the beat. The steps are inspired by African dance moves, a combination of steps from various countries."

"You absolutely captured the soul of the dance. How long does it take to teach that?"

The director chuckled, with a nod to her ankle. "Well, it is not something you can learn tonight."

"I sure want to. It's some of the most exciting, unique, energetic dancing I've seen in a long time."

"The movements are rather contagious, or so I've been told."

"Absolutely. Had my foot not been in this cast, I would have been up dancing! Seriously. I don't know how the rest of the audience stayed in their seats!"

"She's not kidding about the dancing," Julian said. "My girl's a professional dancer. Nicki Long. She was on Broadway before the injury sidelined her."

"For real?"

"A Hair's Tale," Nicki said.

"The lead's best friend." The director pointed at her and held out his hand. "That's where I've seen you before. Ngo Xhe," he introduced himself, pronouncing it "In. Go. Che."

"It's very nice to meet you, Ngo." She returned the enthusiastic handshake. "You've been to the show?"

Ngo shook his head. "I want to. Saw a clip of the show online. I think you guys were on a morning show?"

"Yes, we danced a piece on there."

"You should give me your information. We're fielding a lot of offers across the country from people interested in sponsoring the show. Who knows? We might end up on Broadway."

"Most definitely! I could totally see this show as a hit."

Nicki exchanged information with the young director. There was something about what he'd done that spoke to Nicki and touched her heart in a way she hadn't felt in a very long time. Maybe even since she was a child and first fell in love with dancing. Cast or no, she felt that she could float out of the auditorium and dance to the car.

A half hour later, Nicki and Julian returned to their suite. Tired yet exhilarated after the whirlwind day, she hopped over to the bed and fell back on it.

"Julian!"

"Yes, baby."

"Get over here."

He walked over and sat on the bed, reached down and untied his shoes before crawling on the bed beside her. "Yes, my love."

"Have I told you lately that I love you?"

"I don't remember hearing that lately, no."

"Well, I do. You are amazing. I don't know how you pulled this trip together so quickly, but I can't thank you enough. I've never had an experience like this in my entire life. You made me feel like a princess in a fairy tale."

She wrapped her arms around his neck, pulled his lips toward hers. "Thank you." The first kiss was light, wispy, cushy lips brushing against each other like a whispered promise. Nicki felt Julian press harder, as if he wanted to devour her sweetness. She totally understood and wanted to eat him up, too. They hadn't made love since returning from New York. But she refused to rush the moment. She pulled away from his mouth to lick his ears and nuzzle his neck. She felt him relax, imagined his practiced restraint. He'd gotten the message to follow her lead. Good. Just what she wanted.

Nicki slid her tongue between his parted lips and reached for his belt. He lowered the zipper on the front of her jumpsuit, obviously fine with the direction she headed. She felt a hardening against her thigh. Every part of him was on board. She reached inside his boxers and wrapped cool fingers around a hot, hardening shaft. His hand slid over and beneath the fabric of an OTB original. Tweaked one nipple with his thumb and forefinger while lapping the other with his tongue. Nicki moaned as his hand slid farther down. Felt the love in his touch. The want in his tongue. She wanted it, too. Wanted it now. Wanted to feel his naked goodness against her skin. Thigh to thigh. Chest to breast. Totally connected.

She sat up to undress.

"Here, let me get that for you." Julian kissed her shoulders and the nape of her neck as he eased the jumpsuit away. Continued the oral onslaught as he sought and found the clasp of her bra and loosened that, too. Always a multitasker, the doctor. One of many things that Nicki loved about him.

Once the material was off her shoulders, she lifted her hips. Julian eased the pants down her long, toned legs, ever careful of her ankle as he slid the silky material from even softer skin. His eyes smoldered as he took in dark chocolate nipples that complemented golden tones of caramel skin. He pulled off his shirt and undershirt. Slid off the bed to remove his trousers. His eyes were locked with Nicki's as though mesmerized. She felt powerful. Sexy. Decadent.

Rubbed her hand over the single piece of material that remained on her body. Spread her legs to boldly display what the thong barely hid. His eyes narrowed. Trousers dropped. Boxers followed. His weighty dick swayed gently as he placed a knee on the bed.

"Stop right there, Doctor."

Nicki's moves were graceful, seductive, as she shifted to her knees, bandaged ankle in the air as she crawled toward him. Her eyes dropped from his to the tip of the erection that bobbed its greeting. She licked her lips. Kissed it. Flicked her tongue over the tip. Wrapped her fingers around his long, thick tool. Caressed it lovingly with her fingers. With her tongue. Swirling. Licking. Long wet brushes from base to tip. Grazes of teeth against sensitive skin before lovingly taking him all the way in. He inhaled sharply, began to roll his hips. She felt hands on her butt. Fondling her starfish, making her wet.

"Baby." The word came out on a gush of wind, a gasp when she licked his jewels.

Nicki smiled and turned around. Swayed her butt to tempt a man who didn't need tempting. With the intensity of a soldier directing a heat-seeking missile, she felt Julian ease himself inside her. Slowly, creating delicious friction, pulling out to the tip and plunging in again. He set up a rhythm. She joined in the dance. Julian thrust and stroked again and again. Deeper. Harder. Faster. More. Nicki's body quivered. She went over the edge. Weak legs could no longer hold her. She plopped on her stomach. He followed her down and turned her over. Nicki might have been finished, but Julian was just getting started. He eased his tongue deep into her mouth. Slid his dick in deeply, too. Made love thoughtfully and thoroughly, skillfully, like he did everything else. She remembered his words from earlier, of making new memories. That happened seconds later, as he gave Nicki an orgasm she'd not soon forget.

"Baby, that was amazing."

With one last quick kiss, Nicki turned on her side, scooted back until her body was flush against Julian's and pulled his arm around her waist so they could spoon. She sighed, content in every possible way. Aware of the blessing in this moment. Wonderful afternoon. Fantastic evening. Amazing night. A man who wasn't perfect but who was perfect for her. And as if all that had happened wasn't reason enough to celebrate, there'd been no call or text from Vince. Life was one big hallelujah!

When she'd woke up that morning she'd been sure about returning to New York next week. It had always been home. Was all that she knew. Even being in Los Angeles for her best day ever, she really couldn't see herself living there. But as she heard the steady sound of Julian's deep breathing, signaling sleep, she realized her hard stance toward relocating had softened a bit. She wasn't ready to give notice to her landlord or tear up her MTA card. She knew it would be hard for her to live anywhere but New York. But she knew something else—a woman was allowed to change her mind.

Chapter 18

Julian had a part two planned for his getaway with Nicki, and he'd hoped to have more time off. But an emergency appointment wouldn't allow it. Interrupted his plans. The next morning, after enjoying extra helpings of breakfast and booty in bed, he and Nicki were driven back to the airport. The company plane had been flown back the previous night, so Julian and Nicki boarded the first-class section of a commercial plane just after ten o'clock.

"It's okay, Katie. One o'clock is fine. Right, we're boarding now. I should be in the office around noon. What's after the one o'clock?" He stepped back so that Nicki could take the window seat in the second row, then sat down beside her. "No, thanks," he said to the flight attendant eager to serve him. "Not you, Katie. I was talking to the attendant. Okay, so have her come in at three thirty. Right, I know. That's okay. I'd rather he be allowed to keep his appointment. One o'clock, three thirty and five. Got it. See you soon."

Julian buckled his seat belt, leaned against the seat and closed his eyes.

"Tired much?" Nicki teased.

"Meditating."

"Yeah, right. I should let you catch some sleep. Sounds like your day will be busy."

"A little bit," Julian said through a yawn. "But seeing you happy was worth the loss of sleep."

"I owe you one for sure."

"I plan to collect." Julian repositioned himself so that he could rest his head on Nicki's shoulder. "Don't forget about my mom."

"What about her?"

"You're meeting her for lunch."

"I am?"

He nodded, squeezed her thigh. "She called earlier to reschedule your meeting. I forgot to tell you."

"Are you sure? She said she'd call me."

"She knew you'd be in Los Angeles."

"How long had you planned this?"

"It all happened yesterday. I booked the plane and Dad or someone at the company must have told her. Anyway, you're to meet her at the club at twelve thirty. I'll have the car service pick you up at twelve fifteen. Cool?"

"Sure."

The plane began taxiing down the runway. "Okay, pull that shade, babe. Time to catch forty winks while I can."

Forty winks was all he needed. Shortly before landing, Julian made good use of the hot towels the attendant gave them, along with a cup of strong black joe. He'd planned the trip to Los Angeles all for Nicki, but it had been good for him, too. The laughter. The loving. Nicki's love did that. Was just that powerful. Most women had no idea of their power, of just how completely they could rule a man. He was sure Nicki didn't. Which was probably a good thing. Because the girl had the ability to rock his world. And had.

Upon landing they both took their phones off airplane mode. Indicators dinged and beeped. Julian scrolled through to see what messages he'd missed. Nicki did, too, but only briefly before pulling out her compact and checking her face.

"You're still beautiful," Julian said, not looking up. "Nothing's changed since we left the Ritz."

Nicki kissed his cheek. "You're good for my ego. Think I'll keep you around."

"Is your ego all I'm good for?"

"Not at all. You're a man with many talented weapons. Your mouth is only one of them."

They landed in Oakland. A uniformed driver from the car service stood near the escalator, holding an iPad with "Drake" across the screen. They'd not checked baggage, and airport traffic was light. Within minutes they were settled into a town car's roomy back seat, headed for PC.

Julian pulled out his iPhone and began responding to emails. Nicki rested her head against the seat back and gazed out the window. As they neared Paradise Cove, Julian looked over and was surprised to see a slight frown marring Nicki's brow.

"Babe?" She looked over. "You okay?"

"Yeah, I'm fine."

"Why were you frowning?"

"When?"

"Just now."

"Oh, I didn't realize. Just tired, I guess."

The comment made him smile. "Good loving will do that to you." He reached for her hand. "Hey."

"Yes, love."

"The driver is going to drop me off at the airport to pick up my car. This car can stay with you to drive around PC. All right?"

Nicki looked at her watch. "Sure, that'll be fine. You said lunch is at twelve thirty?" Julian nodded. "Should I wear the OTB mini? Or is that too risqué for the country club's noonday crowd?"

"Depending on who's looking, anything you wear could be considered risqué. You could wear a paper bag and still be sexy."

"Thank you for loving me."

"Easy to do."

They reached the private landing strip, and after a quick

kiss, Julian hopped out and headed directly to his car. He'd kept a calm facade for Nicki's benefit but now couldn't wait to get to his office. Katie had texted that there was a situation involving Claude Johnson—or Dr. Demented, as she liked to call him. He'd chastised her appropriately. Said they were above name-calling. But intuition suggested that whatever awaited him from the doctor would not be good.

Nicki entered the country club just after twelve thirty and hobbled over to the host stand as quickly as the crutches allowed. She'd been told about Jennifer's punctuality and had rushed to get there. Considering the challenges of being injured, and the reason for the frown Julian caught on her face, she was glad to have pulled it together and arrived when she did.

"I'm here for lunch with Mrs. Drake."

"Of course, Ms. Long. One moment and the maître d' will escort you back."

On cue, a handsome older gentleman with salt-and-pepper hair and lively blue eyes appeared at her side, assisted her down the hallway and formally announced her once he'd opened the door to one of the smaller private dining rooms.

"Mrs. Drake, I present your guest, Ms. Long. First courses will arrive shortly."

Jennifer rose gracefully from the chair and walked toward her, arms outstretched. Or floated, Nicki decided, would be a better word. She looked like elegance personified in an ivory pantsuit paired with a navy knit shell and pearl accessories. Nicki was glad she'd changed her mind about wearing the mini and had instead donned a gold, poncho-styled sweaterdress.

"Nicki, darling. Love that dress. You look amazing."

"Thanks, Jennifer."

They shared a brief embrace and walked back to the table set for two.

"Isn't that from Ace's collection?"

"Yes, an original from their fall line. Julian arranged for us to go by their warehouse in LA."

"What a smart and thoughtful move. Especially if he brought me something back. Did he?"

Nicki play cringed. "I don't think so."

"Then I'm afraid there's still some home training to do." Said derisively but with eyes that sparkled with laughter. "You've raised an amazing son."

"He is so very special. Thank you, but honestly, Ike and I can't take all the credit. A lot of what the world sees is Julian being Julian, guided by an inner, almost old-soul knowledge and sensitivity. I'm honored to be his mom."

"I know I was late, by the way. Sorry for that."

"Ah, so you've been warned." Jennifer waved off the comment. "No worries. I completely understand. It must be difficult to navigate the world on crutches."

"I have a whole new appreciation for the disabled. My ankle will be healed in weeks. Can't imagine it being a way of life."

"It is always good to be thankful."

The waiter arrived with warm bread, butter and jams. The ladies shared small talk, mostly on Nicki's ankle and how soon it would heal.

"I never welcome misfortune," Jennifer continued, breaking her bread into bite-size pieces before buttering each individually and placing it daintily in her mouth. "But I must say it's delightful to have you here, and a part of me is hoping you'll stay."

Nicki felt that was a perfect time to eat bread herself. With a mouthful, she couldn't respond.

"I know the chances are quite slim. Yours is a talent that

belongs on Broadway. What I'm hoping, however, is that while you're here, you could help me plan a new component for the community center involving the arts. Specifically music, theater and dance. Unfortunately, the arts have been cut from the budgets of most public schools. I believe they're as important as math or science, maybe more so depending on the child."

"I agree. It's how I honed my craft in those early years and cemented my desire to become a professional dancer. Mom certainly wasn't able to afford private lessons. Those offered through the public school I attended probably helped save my life."

"How so?"

"Kept me off the street, busy, focused. Couldn't dance and be pregnant, so kept me sensible there as well. I think your idea is an excellent one, and I'd be happy to help. Can you share more?"

"The position I have in mind for you is that of artistic director."

Jennifer continued, and for the next hour she and Nicki shared their love of the arts, teaching children and creating dreams. By the time dessert arrived, Nicki had agreed to create a dance curriculum, and while making it clear her goal was to return to Broadway, she did agree to give the AD position some thought. She also promised to stay in Paradise Cove for the duration of her rehabilitation. With Vince and the threatening texts resurfacing, proving to be as hard to shake as the common cold in a New York winter, being on the other side of the country once again seemed like a good idea.

Chapter 19

Julian walked his last patient to the door. "All right, Frank. Good work today."

"Doctor, I can't thank you enough for finally agreeing to see me. I know you wanted me to stay with Johnson. But I tell you something—" The middle-aged man turned around, his eyes shiny with tears. "I feel better with you after one hour than I did with him in ten years."

"I wouldn't discount the work that's been put in to make you better. Often results aren't seen overnight. That being said, your focus should be on the present. Feeling better today. Maintaining a positive outlook today. Where's your journal?"

"Oh, I forgot it in your office."

"Wait right there." Julian went back and retrieved the journal the persistent Frank Snyder had selected, a black faux-leather design with bold white letters stenciled across it: Strive for Progress, not Perfection. "Here you go, Frank. See you next week."

Julian shut the door behind Frank and enjoyed a deep stretch. The day had been long but productive. He was especially pleased with the last appointment. For months he'd declined to treat Frank Snyder, one of the many patients formerly treated by Dr. Claude Johnson who'd practically run to his office and demanded he take them. Actions that undoubtedly led to what had awaited Julian back at the office—a cease and desist letter from Johnson's attorney.

While a bit disappointed, Julian wasn't surprised. He'd hoped Natalie's false allegations had been from her own overactive imagination. But apparently the apple hadn't fallen far from the tree, passing on lies her father obviously believed. Because he wasn't a lawyer, Julian scanned the letter and emailed a copy straight over to Niko's wife, Monique, a tiger in the courtroom before marrying his brother and reducing her workload. The hotshot attorneys were out of town, campaigning in Sacramento, but she promised to look at it once back in their suite. Julian wasn't worried. He'd done nothing wrong. But with people like Johnson, and by extension his daughter, all future interaction would require a paper trail.

He walked back into his office and had just placed his laptop in its carrier bag when he heard the door open. What else had Frank forgotten? He did a quick check around, turned to walk into the reception area and came face-to-face with…Dr. Claude Johnson.

Julian recognized him immediately. He looked older, of course, and shorter than Julian remembered. The piercing gray eyes had dimmed, and the few wisps of blond hair left on top of his head were combed over in an attempt to hide the obvious passage of time.

"Dr. Johnson, hello."

"Who were you expecting, another one of my patients?"

"My client roster is confidential, as you know, but in a town this size I'm sure you're aware of or can deduce that some who've stopped coming to you have made their way to my office. That being said, considering what was delivered by courier today, I wasn't expecting you. Why are you here, and not your attorney?"

"Last I heard it was a free country. Or have the Drakes bought up the entire town and are now handing out passes to walk around?"

Julian had enjoyed an amazing but exhausting twenty-four hours in LA, followed by several hours of intense counseling. Lunch had been a salad at his desk in between patients. He didn't need this right now.

"Dr. Johnson, I've been taught to respect my elders. But this is my private business and you are trespassing. Please see your way to the door."

"Can talk behind my back but not to my face. I figured as much."

"Our inability to converse is entirely your doing, a tone set by what you had delivered today. Any communication between us will now be through our lawyers." Julian walked past Johnson and opened the door. He was done talking. His opening the door was a very clear message.

A shade of red crept up from Johnson's collar, evidence of bottled rage. He reached the door and turned to Julian. "Stop trying to steal my patients. Go out and find your own."

He kept his usual cool, but by the time he arrived home to pick up Nicki for dinner, Julian was in a mood. He tried to hide it from Nicki—wasn't successful. Her first comment as he drove them to the restaurant made it clear.

"We could have ordered in, you know. Or I could have cooked something."

Julian glanced over. "When'd you start cooking?"

"I can cook." Another glance, this one accompanied by a wry smile. "What? I can. I mean, there hasn't been a stint in culinary school so it wouldn't be a five-course meal. But I've perfected a few dishes."

"Name one."

"I'd rather you name what's bothering you."

Julian didn't hesitate. "Claude Johnson."

"Who's that?"

"One of two other therapists in town, the older one who had the market cornered for about thirty years."

"The one whose daughter accused you of stealing clients?"

"You remember that, huh?"

"An old classmate—" she used air quotes "—coming by your office on behalf of her father? Yeah, girlfriends tend to remember ploys like that." Julian recalled Natalie's appearance and actions from that day. The heels and mini, flirty hair and mannerisms. He gave a thoughtful nod. "The doctor, what did he want?"

"I really don't know, especially since a cease and desist from him was what greeted me today when I reached the office." He shared details about the letter, that he'd sent a copy to Monique and the brief conversation with the doctor.

"What did Monique say?"

"She and Niko are in Sacramento on business, so she couldn't check it out right away. She did suggest I create a log of interactions with both him and Natalie, which I did before leaving the office. A man is no better than his reputation. Which is why I refuse to have mine sullied by Johnson's lies."

"It's rare I see you get this worked up, babe. Don't let those haters steal your joy." Nicki reached over to rub Julian's shoulders. "You're a good man, a great therapist, and people around here know it. It'll take more than a couple rumors from a washed-up psychiatrist to change their minds."

They reached Acquired Taste and entered a fuller parking lot than expected, given it was a weeknight. Julian pulled into one of two reserved parking spaces, helped Nicki into the restaurant, then moved the car to a regular spot. When he returned, a menu, a shot of premium tequila and a saucer of accompaniments were on his place mat. The same sat in front of Nicki. He looked at her with a raised brow.

"To take the edge off," she replied with a smile. "Because neither of us are drinkers, I figured one shot is all we'll need."

He sniffed it, bunched up his nose. "What is this, gasoline?"

"Close. Enough to smooth out our ride but not rev up our engines."

"What if I want to get your engine revved up?"

"Baby, you can do that with a single look or a simple kiss. Those scrumptious lips, long curly lashes around those bedroom eyes…" She licked her lips seductively and lowered her voice. "It's happening right now. I'm getting hot. And wet."

Julian's arm shot up as he looked around. "Check, please!"

"Ha! You're a sex fiend."

"Yes."

She held up her shot glass. "Let's toast to sex fiends, and how much I love the one currently sitting across from me."

"Wait." Julian nodded toward the saucer. "What's all this for?"

"Oh, right. There's an art to this. So, we're supposed to place a little of the salt on our tongue, drink the shot straight down and follow up with a bite of the lemon slice. The salt and citric acid will cut the tequila's burn. So wet your finger—" she licked her forefinger "—like this." Julian licked his finger. "Now stick it in the salt."

Again, he complied.

"Now, you lick the salt off my finger and I'll lick…well, for now, I'll lick your finger."

Julian smiled broadly. "Stop that nasty talk. It's making me uncomfortable."

"A little too much for my conservative doctor?"

"A lot to try to keep calm between my legs."

"Ah, got it."

She held out her finger. He placed his near her lips. Each licked the other's finger. Julian's action was straightforward. Nicki took longer, swirled her tongue around Julian's pointer and suckled as she eased it from her mouth.

They picked up their glasses, downed the tequila and bit the lemon. With closed eyes Julian absorbed the tequila's heat and the lemon's tartness. A few seconds later he smiled. "That wasn't too bad."

Nicki's face told a different story. Her eyes were scrunched, her lips pulled into a grimace. She finally spoke, her voice low and raspy. "That burned everything from my mouth to my anus."

At that very moment the waiter arrived. "May I take your order?"

"Ooh!" Nicki started after the question. "I thought he was going to offer to take something else."

Nicki and Julian cracked up.

So into themselves they took little note of who dined around them. For two women in particular, the oblivion fit perfectly into their plan. A few choice snaps and they left unnoticed, their targets not knowing they'd been there at all.

The next morning Julian woke up to texts from his siblings and a missed call from Jennifer, all regarding a picture making its way across the web and a story on the gossip blog *Ask Ashley* titled Dancer Dates Drunk Doctor?

Chapter 20

The Drake clan circled the wagons. Sunday brunch got moved to Friday night. Attendance wasn't mandatory. Didn't need to be. When Jennifer called, the clan came. Being out of town was the lone reason one would be absent. London and Ace were doing a show in Dubai. Niko's narrow lead in the polls and crisscross campaigning across the state meant he and Monique wouldn't be there, but that didn't stop their making an important contribution. In addition to the response she'd written for the cease and desist letter from Dr. Johnson, she'd given Julian legal options for dealing with Ashley's gossip.

Julian and Nicki were there with his parents, Ike Jr. and Quinn, Warren and Charli, Terrell and Aliyah, and Teresa and Atka. The table had been set informally, the household staff sent home to enjoy their weekend off. Jennifer entered the dining room bearing two trays, a very pregnant Charli waddling behind her. Julian hopped up to take the bowl from his expecting sister-in-law.

"I've got this, Doctor," Charli replied, batting his hand away.

"Are you sure?" Terrell asked.

"Bro, you took the words right out of my mouth."

"Mine, too," Quinn and Aliyah chimed together.

Everyone laughed. The women set down the evening's first course—jalapeño–and–goat cheese hush puppies, stuffed artichokes, and spicy chile crostini with a variety of sauces.

Terrell accepted a tray from his mom, removed a stuffed artichoke and then passed it on. "Is the third time the charm, making this the last little dogie for the ranch, sis?"

"I beg your pardon." Charli acted appropriately incensed.

"What? Y'all are ranchers. I thought a pet name quite appropriate."

"Then call him a kid, but not a dogie. God's will, he'll be neither motherless nor neglected."

"Oh, is that what the word means? My bad."

"Simple city-dweller ignorance," Charli said, nonplussed, as she filled her plate with a serving of each appetizer. She picked up a stuffed artichoke and smiled. "You're forgiven."

"You need to serve Quinn some of whatever you're drinking. It's time for me to pass on the name and usher in Ike III."

"Yes, and give some to Aliyah," Terrell added. "We're going to have a baseball team, so best get started."

"Easy for the man to say," Aliyah said. "Let's get you through that first one's midnight feedings and diaper changes and then see how you're talking."

The first courses were removed. Teresa helped Jennifer bring out piping-hot bowls of seafood chowder, flown in from a favored New Hampshire restaurant just that morning. Jennifer set down the last bowl and took her seat. She immediately reached for the soupspoon for a taste.

"Delicious."

The others followed suit and agreed.

"I'd have you all over every night if I could," she continued between spoonfuls of soup. "But there is a specific reason I invited you over tonight."

"Ask Ashley," Aliyah answered quickly.

Terrell lifted his linen napkin and sat back as he wiped his mouth. "I told y'all how to handle her when she started tripping years ago. Money. Give her some money to shut her up or threaten her livelihood to shut her down."

Jennifer emitted an uncharacteristic humph. "What livelihood?"

"Exactly," Teresa said. "What we need to do is give her a taste of her own medicine." Teresa ran a successful blog with a million opt-in readers.

Terrell looked up surprised. "Not on your blog."

"Why not?"

"Because the name of your blog is *Tip-Top Taste*. Ashley has none."

The men chuckled.

"Attention is what she wants," Aliyah said.

"Craves," Warren added.

Teresa stirred her soup. "She tries to push our buttons because we ignore her."

Jennifer agreed. "Precisely. Not quite the effect we were seeking."

"Perhaps," Nicki said. "But I agree that we shouldn't give her any of our energy. Unless it's in the form of a Brooklyn beat down like the bullies in grade school."

"That's what I'm talking about!" Aliyah laughed and raised her hand to high-five. As a native New Yorker, she totally understood.

Julian cleared his throat. "Sorry to break up the New York lovefest, ladies. But there will be no fisticuffs. That's not the way we Drakes like to make the news."

"What do you suggest, son?" asked Ike Sr.

"That we send a letter to both the blog and the company that hosts it demanding an apology and retraction, threatening to take legal action if our order is ignored. That was Monique's suggestion, the same as she gave when it came to the doctor, and in that case it seems to have worked very well."

It was true. The day after Dr. Johnson's unexpected visit, Monique took over. She'd taken affidavits of support from the patients who'd chosen Julian as their therapist. His notes were transcribed and filed along with his letters recommending to some that they stay with their current doctor. Finally, she'd expressed Julian's desire not to have unexpected visits to his office by either Dr. Johnson or Natalie. He'd not seen or heard from either since.

Teresa stood to help Jennifer gather the soup bowls. "I don't know, I'm kind of leaning toward that Brooklyn-style beat down."

Julian's sensible solution prevailed. He texted a note to Monique right from the dinner table. The conversation shifted from gossip to Gallup polls and what each family member could contribute to ensure Niko's win. As they left the estate, Jennifer reminded Nicki about their meeting on Monday. Problems solved or at least addressed, the dancer and doctor spent a quiet weekend making more memories.

That Monday, Nicki left the town house feeling optimistic. She'd had a phone consultation with Dr. Allen, which was very welcome good news. He told her if the bone had set and begun to heal, the cast could be removed. She'd still have to wear an Aircast or boot, but at least she'd be able to rent a car to get around instead of being chauffeured. Not that she didn't enjoy the perks of having a car at the ready, transportation a mere phone call away to take her wherever she desired. But she also liked being independent and looked forward to being able to check out the town and surrounding communities on her own.

She adjusted the shoulder strap on her oversize bag, secured her crutches and walked out of the house.

"You got it, Miss Nicki?"

"Yes, thank you, Devante." He opened the car door. "And what did I tell you about calling me 'miss'? I thought we handled that last week during the drive to the club."

"I'm sorry mi—I mean, Nicki." His nervous laugh revealed straight white teeth set in the handsome face of a man she guessed to be in his early twenties. He closed her door softly, then hurried around to the other side of the car. "To the community center, right?"

"That's right. How far is it?"

"Ten minutes or less." He backed out of the drive and headed toward the town's main drag.

"Not far at all."

"No, ma'am. Nothing is really far in this town."

She didn't correct him this time, though the formal title made her feel old. She knew he was only being respectful. "Where are you from, Devante? With those 'miss' and 'ma'am' manners, I'd guess down south. But you don't have an accent."

Another smile. "No. I'm not from down south."

He was cute. A good kid. She liked him. "Where, then? You seem to know your way around the city, but I get the feeling you're not from here."

He eyed her through the rearview mirror. "I'm from LA."

"Ah, that's where the city swagger comes from. I didn't think you'd grown up here."

"Is that a good thing?"

"Swagger? Oh, yeah. Definitely. Have you ever been to New York?"

"No. I've never been out of California."

"Wow, really? You'll have to get out and see a little bit of the world."

"One of these days."

"How'd you get here, if you don't mind me asking?"

"To PC?"

"Yes."

"Flew in on Southwest Airlines. Then it was straight down the 101 to the 77."

She met his twinkling eyes in the rearview mirror with a smirk and a shrug. "Hey, I'm not trying to get in your business. Just making conversation with one of the few people in this town who seems to be real, unlike some of the fake, shallow people I've run across." Her thoughts were on Ashley and the link Paige had sent to the misleading blog post highlighting Julian and Nicki's Thursday night dinner at Acquired Taste. The story had been picked up by a New York–based blogger and by Monday had even gotten a mention on a national network. Ashley had gotten some of the attention she wanted. That it was from a story based on a thinly veiled lie, Nicki thought, a bit sadly, probably didn't matter to her at all.

"So you've checked that out, too, huh?" Devante waited for a car to pass, then turned left onto one of only four major thoroughfares in all of Paradise Cove. "You know Monique, the mayor's wife?" Devante clucked and shook his head. "What am I saying? Of course you do."

"Yes, I know her, though not very well."

"You know she's an attorney, right?"

"Yes."

"She used to practice in LA. Around the same time I was being a hardhead, getting into trouble, trying to prove my manhood and other stupid stuff. She saved me. Kept me from a long lockdown, know what I'm saying?"

"Out of prison?"

He nodded. "Brought me up here. A whole different world from where I came from. Mr. Niko started mentoring me. Then Mr. Terrell and Mr. Ike Sr., they all helped show me what a real man looked like."

Devante turned into the parking lot of the community center. He pulled up to the entrance, but Nicki continued the conversation. Just when she thought she'd seen it all, the Drakes found another way to impress her. "You work for one of them now?"

"I'm going to college full-time and work for them part-time running errands, driving, cleaning the center, whatever they want me to do."

"What's your major?"

"Criminal justice. Want to be able to help some other young guys the way Monique and the Drakes helped me."

"You're clearly a good man, even if you did some bad things. I'm glad the system didn't claim you."

"That's for sure. It's claimed too many. Here, let me get that door for you."

Nicki tipped a reluctant Devante, thinking that the criminal system often punished good men like him when jerks like Vince got to walk around free. Some bad apples could do just about anything, could go anywhere they wanted. Which for Nicki would soon present a problem even more bothersome than the *Ask Ashley* blog.

Chapter 21

Nothing could dim Nicki's outlook that Monday. She left the Drake Community Center feeling better than she'd felt since her date with a runaway bike. Her mood was so bright she had Devante stop at the new organic grocer. Julian had doubted she knew her way around a kitchen, but she planned to show him a thing or two. He'd arrived at the center shortly after she left, had called while she scanned fresh veggies. Told her what time he expected to arrive home. Asked what she wanted him to bring home. Her answer didn't require him to stop anywhere. She didn't even need tequila.

An hour later, freshly showered and changed, Nicki stepped back and admired her handiwork. Jennifer had scoffed at Nicki's choice of black china, but Nicki's taste often went against the grain. She liked how the dark backdrop made the colors of her simple salad pop. The dark green spinach, red cherry tomatoes and yellow sweet peppers drizzled with a creamy homemade vinaigrette. Walking past the dining room area into the kitchen, she lifted the lid of a cast-iron pot. Inhaling the mixture brought out a big smile. The Italian sausage and fresh herbs in the cheesy tortellini dish gave off a highly complex aroma. Who'd know that she'd used words like *fast* and *easy* when searching for something to show off her limited cooking skills? Certainly not Julian. If he wasn't properly impressed with her homemade dinner, then her outfit and the dessert she planned to serve bedside would certainly raise her score.

Nicki poured herself a glass of sparkling juice, picked up her cell phone from the kitchen island and walked into the living room to catch the news. Normally not much of a TV watcher and totally uninterested in politics, she'd been drawn into the California senatorial race and watched nightly results along with every other Drake in the States. She clicked the remote and switched to a local station. Minutes into watching an editorial piece comparing Niko and the rest of the candidates, her message indicator pinged.

She tapped her phone, still focused on the announcer, who seemed to offer a balanced, unbiased perspective on those running for office. She looked down. Unknown number. The same message that had showed when Vince's texts started up again the day she met Jennifer for lunch. Her heart sank. *Please don't let it be him. Not here. Not now.* Begrudgingly, she opened the text.

So you're in Paradise Cove with your doctor boyfriend and his rich clique. Looks like the nerd doctor has a wild side! Went online and checked out the town. Quaint, upscale, a bit on the small side. But perhaps a perfect place to get away from these fools still jocking me about the money I owe. Saying they're now going to start charging interest. Lucky for me the timing might be perfect. If I come there will you show me around?

Nicki tossed down the phone in disgust. She'd show him around, all right. Show him the main road that led out of town. She tried to refocus on the news show. Hard to do with Vince's words running around in her head.

"He wouldn't come here. That party boy? No way." Nicki's shoulders relaxed. Easy breathing returned. Ten minutes in a place like Paradise Cove, and Vince would be bored to death.

Jennifer was known as a magician and miracle worker, able to pull off the impossible time and again. But what

Julian witnessed at the community center when he crossed paths with his girl increased his regard for his mother. Exponentially. He was just about ready to put her on par with a saint. The Nicki he'd fallen in love with had come out of the dark.

He'd first noticed a change after Nicki and Jennifer's country-club lunch date. She'd greeted him that night with a light in her eyes, an excitement that he'd only seen before when discussing her passion or just after she got hired for a Broadway show. An excitement that emanated like fire from her body that scorched and sizzled when they made love. For the first time in six years, the very first time, Julian had allowed himself to truly believe. To actually entertain the idea that his girl—the woman who stole his heart the first time he saw her dancing across campus to a song in her head that only she heard—might leave New York and move to Paradise Cove. He hadn't felt this optimistic since…since that magical night in Times Square. That was the best time ever. Until it wasn't. Until she clarified what her hug under the flashing neon lights meant. That she didn't want to embarrass him, but she didn't want to marry him, either.

As Julian entered the parking lot of the Drake Community Center and pulled into one of the reserved spaces, his joy had dropped a bit. There was room for optimism, but maybe not a dance in the end zone. Then he'd arrived at the center and saw that light in her eyes. Against his will and self-delivered admonitions not to, that optimistic belief bubbled up again.

Walking into the center, he passed the administrative offices, waved at Miss Marva and continued to Terrell's office farther down the hall. He tapped the open door.

"Come on in, JuJu." Terrell greeted him as he typed on his laptop.

Julian's expression was a cross between a smile and a wince. "Cut out that bull crap. I hated when you called me that as a kid."

"And as an adult?"

"I hate it even more." They both laughed at that. Julian plopped into one of the leather chairs facing Terrell's desk.

"I thought you were here for a therapy session."

"I am."

"With Lopez?"

Julian shook his head. "Marion, the kid from Sacramento."

Terrell stopped typing. Swiveled his chair around to face Julian. "Marion Tucker. Moved here to live with his aunt. Real chip on his shoulder, that kid."

"That chip is a shield. You know why he moved here, right?"

Terrell nodded. "I'm glad you're here to help him, bro."

"Me, too. I'm told he hasn't been the same since his best friend got killed. And right in front of him? Stray bullet fired from an officer's gun?"

"That's why his aunt petitioned the court for temporary custody, to try to save his life. She's got a difficult journey ahead of her."

"There's still time. Fourteen is an extremely critical age for any youth, but especially for today's young black male. He's a tough case. Lots of anger, sadness, pain. But it's not too late to save him. The aunt bringing him to a smaller town from a big city was a good move. Less distractions and opportunities for trouble. Even better that she brought him here, where he can see positive male role models."

"Speaking of role models, remember me telling you that I was going to place an ad on CarlsList for an athletic director?"

"No, I don't remember. Doesn't mean you didn't tell me, though."

"Yeah, that's right. With Nicki around you tend to not think straight."

"Yeah, whatever, man."

Terrell chuckled. "Well, I did. Posted it there in the hopes of attracting someone from the bigger cities—San Jose, Sacramento, even Oakland."

"And?"

"I got interest from a big city, all right. All the way out East."

"Really? Who?"

"Vince Edwards."

Julian thought for a moment. "The basketball player?" Terrell nodded. "He's living here?"

"Not yet. But he's checking the town out as a definite possibility."

"But he's East Coast, Philly—hated the West Coast during his playing years."

"I think what he hated was the Lakers and that whooping the guards put on him every time he came to town."

"Ha! That's probably true. I'm surprised he was looking at CarlsList."

"Tell me about it. And even so, I'm surprised he was looking for jobs on the West Coast. Guess you have to follow the money, and goodness knows he burned enough bridges back in his playing days to need a scenery change."

"How long has he been out of the game? Four, five years?"

"Something like that. Did a little search after the call. Read that he played a couple seasons over in Europe. Got into tax trouble with the IRS. Had to file bankruptcy. Lost that big old house featured on *Ballers Got Bank*. Remember that?"

"No, and from the sound of it, that's a good thing. Damn. It's a shame to make the kind of money he did and end up broke."

"Without proper financial guidance, it's the only thing that can happen. You can't learn how to manage money if you've never had any."

"Is he coming in for an interview?"

Terrell nodded. "Next week. Could be a good addition to the center. He's been out of the league for a while, but he's still a star to the kids."

"A star, maybe, but not necessarily a good role model. If he was, he'd still be playing instead of being a talented but poisoned point guard no one wants to sign."

"I thought about that, but he's older. Wiser. Figured there'd be no better way to show what not to do than somebody like him whose questionable choices cost him millions of dollars and a career. He grew up poor, troubled, like Marion and many of the other kids this center serves. They'll listen to someone like him."

"You know Mom talked to Nicki, wants her to be the center's artistic director."

"Is that a possibility?"

"Looks like it might be."

"I didn't think Miss Broadway could breathe for too long outside New York's air."

Julian summoned up his best Terrell impression. "I'm giving her a special kind of oxygen."

"Wow. Just say no, okay?"

Julian grinned broadly. "I did you pretty good, huh?"

"Keep your day job, JuJu."

Julian stood and headed to the door. "Uh-huh. Call me that again, and I'll tell Aliyah about the time down at Grandpa's when you thought Teresa's jump rope was a snake and peed the bed."

"On that note, Dr. Drake, I believe your counseling session begins shortly."

"I thought so."

Nicki heard a car in the driveway and the garage door raising a few seconds later. She turned off the TV and, ignoring the crutches, hopped into the dining room and lit two tapered candles placed on either side of a vase of fresh sunflowers. The door from the garage opened as she reached the dimmer. As Julian turned the corner, the lights faded.

His stop was abrupt, almost midstride. "Wow."

"Like my outfit?"

She watched the slow sweep of Julian's eyes over her body. "I love it."

A squiggle of excitement flip-flopped in her gut. Julian walked over to where she stood by the dimmer. Reached out and fingered the nearly sheer minidress made of silky organza. Slid his arms around her waist and pulled her close.

"I love you."

He kissed her. Pulled back and kissed her again. Soon tongues dueled. Nipples pebbled. Sexes dewed and stiffened.

"The food," Nicki murmured, pulling away. "I made tortellini."

"You made it. Like, cooked it?"

"All by myself. And set a beautiful table, which you haven't mentioned, by the way." She swept her hand across the room. "The mood I've set. The romantic atmosphere."

Julian turned and took in the plated salad. The flowers and dim light. "It's real nice, baby, but can I be honest? From the moment I turned the corner, all I saw was you."

He wrapped her in his arms again.

"Good answer, Doctor." Nicki deftly escaped him and

walked toward the stove. "Good tactic, too. But you'll have to eat dinner before getting dessert."

Dinner was scrumptious. Dessert was even better. Nicki forgot that Vince had texted. The ex-ballplayer being interviewed to work at the center never entered Julian's mind. All on the lovers' minds that night was each other.

But that same night, on the other side of the country, the doctor and dancer were very much on someone else's mind.

Chapter 22

The next morning, Nicki was up before Julian. A rarity. But after waking sometime shortly after the birds, ideas for the community center's arts program began to fuel her passion and chased sleep away. Plus, her ankle was healing. A clear cure for the doldrums. She'd put a little weight on it late last night. Not for long, and there'd been discomfort, but that she could at all was a clear sign of progress. That and the lessening need for pain medication. She'd gone the whole weekend without a pill. The haze receded, and when she went into the bathroom for a quick shower and looked in the mirror, she felt and saw her true self for the first time in weeks.

Downstairs she put on water for tea, then sat on a tall chair at the island and turned on her tablet. She started a search for nearby dance colleges with artistic programs. She and Jennifer hadn't discussed an overall budget for the program or even specifics about what she would be paid. Even if there were no funds currently available, Nicki still believed she could find talented students in college programs willing to teach for credit and experience. She quickly found several that offered degrees in theater, dance and performance. Perfect for the artistic mediums she suggested first be offered at the center—theater, music and dance. She focused on those closest to Paradise Cove, found the email addresses to who she thought were the appropriate faculty and began formulating an introductory letter.

The kettle whistled. Julian ambled down the stairs and entered the kitchen just as she poured a cup.

"Tea?" she asked, still holding the kettle.

He walked over and kissed her forehead. "Got any with caffeine?"

"Green tea. Even better."

"I believe it, if that's what has you looking so perky." He slumped into the chair next to Nicki's tablet and suppressed a yawn. "Why are you up so early?"

"Couldn't sleep. Working on the dance curriculum for the center has me all excited. Working with others in the art is the next best thing to dancing myself."

He nodded toward the tablet. "Can I look?"

"Sure." She bought the covered mugs over and set them on the table. "I'm looking for college students as teachers who might work for credit instead of pay."

"Thinking like a true nonprofiteer, babe."

"I've gone through life on a shoestring budget. Can pinch Lincoln off a penny and Roosevelt off a dime."

Julian took a moment and read what Nicki had written so far. "Who's this letter that you're drafting for?"

"Faculty members at the schools I've chosen—Santa Rosa Junior, University of the Pacific and both San Jose and Sacramento State." Nicki poured agave and lemon juice into the cups. "I'm also thinking about tapping into the community of retired artists for people who can mentor as well as teach."

"Speaking of mentoring and teaching, guess who might be heading up our athletic department?"

"Who?"

"You might not even know the name, since you're not into sports. A former pro basketball player named Vince Edwards."

Nicki almost spewed out her Citrus Sunshine and wished she could be so lucky. She also wished she could respond, say something witty. Or even better, something real. Clearly this was the moment of truth. But if she told him,

then what? They'd call off the interview? Which would in-
cite what kind of reaction from Vince? One where he told
Julian what Nicki had failed to disclose? She should have
told him everything as soon as it happened. She realized
that, but now the timing sucked.

"Nicki, did you hear me?"

"Hmm, sorry babe, got distracted. Something about a
basketball player coming to the center?"

Julian swiped a finger over Nicki's cheek as he slid off
the school. "Never mind, babe. I have to get going, but we
can talk later. That tea was good, but tomorrow I'll expect
the chef to serve breakfast."

Nicki laughed as she got up and walked him to the door.
"One good meal and I'm a chef now?"

"You are in my book." He pressed his lips against hers
in a quick kiss. "It's good to see my Nicki back. Love you,
baby."

"Love you, too."

Nicki held her poise until Julian had backed out of the
driveway and started down the street. Then she let out an
anguished sound of frustration, a cross between a growl
and a screech. The interview must have been scheduled
before he'd texted her yesterday. The community center
looking for an athletic director was the perfect timing of
which Vince spoke.

She'd never thought much about reincarnation but Nicki
felt she had to have done something heinous in another
lifetime. Like murder. It could only be karma from some
egregious past wrong that would have put her and Vince
Edwards in the same place, at the same time, right after
she and Julian had broken up. Then have him ask for her
number, and worse, for her to give it to him? Seemed like a
good idea at the time. Hindsight revealed she couldn't have
been more wrong. Now he was coming to Paradise Cove,

turning what she'd thought might be a heavenly situation after all into the pits of hell.

She picked up her phone and scrolled to the last unknown number. Trying to dial it back didn't work. She hit star sixty-nine. That didn't work, either. Crazy that the one time she actually wanted to talk to him, the jerk could not be reached.

She let out another groan followed by a few choice expletives. Then she reached for her phone and checked the time. Just after nine thirty, the screen indicated. Half past noon in New York. She called Paige.

"Please answer," she mumbled, pushing the speaker button and nervously tapping her foot while the phone rang.

"Nicki, hi!"

"I can't get rid of him" was her greeting.

"Huh. Who? What?"

"Vince Edwards. The asshole. I can't figure out what I've done to deserve this type of punishment. I date the guy for a month. Do a show in Atlanta that just happens to be directed by some distant relative, and all of a sudden I owe him a favor."

"Twenty thousand favors."

"To be exact."

"According to him."

"Who does that? And why did he ask me? Why didn't he ask one of his rich baller friends? His mother or father? A bank? I thought extortion was just about the worst he could do, but guess what? He can go even lower. I'm seriously about to lose it, Paige. Why won't he leave me alone!"

"Whoa, Nick. You're scaring me. Slow down. Start over. Tell me what's going on."

"Vince is coming to Paradise Cove."

"Holy crap, Nick! That's crazy!"

"Yeah, because *he's* crazy."

"You didn't have the money here. What makes him think you'll have it there? Julian? He wants you to get it from him?"

"Clearly his main goal is to ruin my life." She told Paige about the community center expansion and the athletic director position. "I can't believe he even saw it. Though he is handy with a computer and the internet. He told me that himself. And thanks to *Ask that A-hole Ashley*, he knew where I was."

"From there he could have put any one of several word combinations in the search engine and pulled up that ad. What is Julian saying? He's cool under pressure but this has got to have him pissed." Nicki sighed and leaned against the island counter. "Nicki…you did tell Julian about Vince, right? Yeah, you told me you did."

"I told him about a guy I dated briefly trying to extort money. I didn't go into detail."

"He doesn't know it's Vince?"

"I didn't think it was important."

"Do you think it's important now? Like, before he gets to Paradise Cove. Before the interview? Before something crazy happens, like he gets the job. Something crazy like that. I don't get why you're being so tight-lipped about this. You already told him you dated."

"But I didn't say I slept with him."

"So what? You and Julian were broken up. You were an adult on a date. It's what we do. Tell him, Nick."

"I already hurt him so badly when I turned him down. To know I was with another guy when we were only broken up a month? It'll really upset him, Paige. Especially now, since it's information I withheld when sharing the rest. Julian isn't like the other guys. Sex isn't a casual thing with him."

"Then what are you going to do? Roll the dice and hope Vince doesn't get the job?"

Nicki stood straight as an idea came to her. "Maybe I can get him to not need it. Thanks for being a sounding board, girl. I gotta go."

"Nick—"

Too late. She'd already pushed the end button. Before she could think herself out of the tricky yet possible solution that had popped in her head, she called Jennifer.

"Hi, Jennifer. It's Nicki."

"Hello, Nicki. How are you?"

"I'm okay, thanks. I was calling about the artistic director position."

"Yes?"

"While my long-term plan is to return to Broadway, and I want to make that very clear, I am now giving serious consideration to the position you offered."

"Nicki, that's wonderful!"

"I can only make a one-year commitment. Are you okay with that?"

"Absolutely. You can get the program up and running and hire an assistant to take over the reins. Have you told Julian?"

"No, I just decided."

"I'm so happy, Nicki. He will be thrilled!"

"I know—can't wait to tell him. Until then, can we keep this between us?"

"Of course. I wouldn't want to ruin this very special surprise."

"Um, there's another question I need to ask, and this one is a bit awkward."

"What is it, dear?"

"I need the specifics regarding salary, if you don't mind."

"Of course, Nicki. How remiss of me not to have included that in the discussion. It's not along the lines of what someone with your experience and renown is worth, I'm afraid. The starting salary we're offering is only thirty-five thousand annually, but there are perks, including a five-thousand-dollar signing bonus over and above the annual compensation."

Jennifer continued detailing the benefits, which included comprehensive health insurance and paid vacation days. Those facts barely registered. Nicki didn't hear much past the words *five thousand*. She wrapped up the conversation and ended the call. Her next move was going to be trying to reach Vince to make him a five-thousand-dollar offer she hoped he wouldn't refuse.

Chapter 23

She sent Vince a text with a payment plan. Five thousand now, and five more for the next three months. He didn't reply. A second text and again, nothing. She learned the one thing worse than hearing from Vince Edwards was not hearing from the extorter at all. Not knowing his movements. If he'd considered her offer. When or if he still planned a trip to PC.

When she finally received a text a few days later, his answer wasn't what she wanted—he said no, with a smiley face and a LOL. He countered, once again demanding the whole twenty grand. She countered back and offered ten. It would take going into her savings and her first couple checks. Didn't matter. Right now his absence was more important than a nest egg. He wanted her to wire the money. She wanted him to sign off on it first. Have it in writing that he'd no longer harass her, he wouldn't come west and she'd pay him in full.

That exchange had happened days ago. He'd never responded. Her stomach nerves had been coiled ever since, in knots tight enough to puke. Couldn't let the feelings show now, though. She'd signed the agreement to become the community center's artistic director. Today's Sunday brunch was being held in her honor at the country club instead of the Drake estate. Time to put on a positive game face. All eyes would be on her.

"How do I look?"

Julian took in the simple dress that on Nicki's toned, curvy body looked elegant and chic. The deep cranberry color brought out the golden tones of her skin. The curly black locks usually kept bound were loose, framing her face and tickling her shoulders. A low-slung belt accented her small waist, and its gold trim was complemented by the jewelry she wore.

"You look beautiful, babe. I feel like the shy, nerdy kid who snagged the cute, hot girl and wondered how he got so lucky."

"You sure? I'm nervous."

"Really?"

"A little bit."

"Why? It's going to be mostly family there."

"I know. But today it becomes official. I'm going to be here for at least a year."

While the Friday night dinner had closely resembled it, Nicki had avoided the famed Drake Sunday brunch. Having been in their town a month, this was a fete, and a calculated one at that. Individually, each Drake exuded a certain type of power and confidence. As a group they could be quite intimidating, especially for someone like Nicki, who'd grown up an only child and cherished her privacy. That she and Julian had dated for two years before she met the family had gotten her labeled "the invisible girlfriend" and made the first meeting awkward. It had taken that long for her to admit she was actually in a relationship, something she'd sworn wouldn't happen. Her first and only love was dancing. Until Julian Drake walked into her life.

"Baby, why are you tripping? You know everybody. You'll be fine."

"Yes, but I'm not used to seeing everybody at once."

"What about the other Friday?"

"That wasn't the whole dynasty!"

"Ah, come on now. We're not so bad."

"Easy for you to say. You're a Drake."

"I could easily make it happen for you to be one, too." He glanced over, waited. She remained silent. "I tried that once before. You weren't ready." He waited for an answer. "Nothing to say?"

"You already said it. I wasn't ready. I grew up dreaming about being a dancer. Guess I never thought about being a wife."

"And now?"

"I still haven't thought much about it."

"Maybe you should."

With a last look in the mirror, Nicki reached for her purse. "Come on, babe. We should go. I don't want to be late."

She reached out to smooth his lapel.

"I love that you picked a shirt that matches my dress. Love that color on you, too." She leaned over, kissed his cheek. "Who knew a man with glasses could be so sexy?"

"You know what they say. The sexiest muscle on a man is his brain."

"That isn't what poked me in the back this morning."

"Touché."

A short time later they reached the Paradise Cove Country Club. Julian pulled up to the valet, and they were soon ushered into the large private dining room, beautifully decorated in autumn shades. Deep purple cloths and pumpkin-colored linen adorned three round tables. On them were settings of white china and Waterford crystal goblets trimmed in gold, eight settings per table. Elaborate bouquets with fresh autumn flowers were in six-foot-tall vases. The room was stunning. Perfect. Surpassed only by the beautiful people casually chatting inside—the Northern California Drakes and a handful of choice supporters. Nicki was glad to learn she'd been seated with Terrell and his wife. Their shared New York background had created an instant affinity. Nicki appreciated Aliyah's East Coast authenticity, and with Terrell at the table there would never be silence or boredom.

As waiters unobtrusively served the first course, Jennifer stood to address the room. "Good Sunday, family."

"Good Sunday."

"As many if not most of you already know, the past week has been one of awesome progress for the Drakes, our community center and Paradise Cove. Ike and I would like to publicly thank Wayne and Lillian Channing—" she nodded toward them "—our dear friends, longtime neighbors and staunch supporters of Niko's political career. Last week's polls calmed my nerves and alleviated Ike's ulcer a bit, as Niko's lead reached double digits." The room applauded. "The news is encouraging but we can't ease up. Son, no matter what happens, know that you have been an exemplary mayor of Paradise Cove and a stellar example of true leadership. We're so very proud of you.

"I am also delighted to make official an addition to our family. Oops," Jennifer hurriedly continued with mock dismay. "I meant faculty—to the Drake Community Center faculty." The room joined her in laughter. Julian placed a firm arm around Nicki as Jennifer pointed out, "Nicki Long."

Applause and whistles followed.

"Until recently Nicki was a lead dancer on Broadway, starring in the hit show *A Hair's Tale*."

Jennifer was interrupted by a ringing cell phone.

"Hold up, Mom," Terrell blurted. "That might be Broadway calling her back!"

"Don't answer," Jennifer pleaded dramatically. "Please, don't answer!"

Humored responses and chuckles followed as an embarrassed Nicki hurriedly reached for her clutch, pulled out the phone and silenced it.

"Is everything okay?" Jennifer asked. Nicki nodded. "Good, because unfortunately a few weeks ago, that was not the case. Nicki was injured in a bicycle accident and was forced to leave the show. Paradise Cove and our center are the grateful beneficiaries of her misfortune, as she has just signed on to a yearlong term as Drake Community Center's artistic director."

Nicki forced a smile as the diners applauded. She felt Julian's arm slide around her shoulders and tried to find comfort within the embrace. Tried to present a cheery, peaceful demeanor despite the text she'd glimpsed just seconds before. From Vince. Four short words that stabbed her heart like a knife.

See you in PC.

Chapter 24

In his next text, he agreed to take the money. Added he was still coming to town. The center had paid for the flight. Her nerves became so frayed that simple breathing was difficult. How did criminals operate without having a breakdown? Between the covert back-and-forth text exchanges with Vince and assuring an astute Julian she was okay, Nicki was almost ready for a shot of tequila. Instead, she turned her mind to more positive news. Like how within a few hours her cast would be gone. And perhaps convincing Paige to come out for a visit. *A Hair's Tale* was nearing the end of its first run and Paige had never been to PC.

Julian flopped on his back, barely awake. "You sure you don't want me to stay and go with you?"

"No, thank you, babe. You've been amazing these past four weeks. I've been coddled and spoiled and a part of me could get used to that. But that independent part that you love so much is screaming for control!"

"That sounds like you're still going to rent a car."

"I am. For a whole week, at least!"

Nicki watched Julian get out of bed and walk into the bathroom shaking his head. She couldn't see the problem. He wanted to run out and buy her a car. She wanted time to try out different models and find which model fit her, what style she wanted. She also wanted to secure a loan and make the payments instead of allowing Julian to plunk down a big stack of cash. Julian didn't know that part. He already did so much, basically took care of everything. Nicki appreciated everything he did but wanted to be a bit self-reliant. With her five-thousand-dollar advance going to el jerko, money was going to be tight. Of course, Julian didn't know that, either. Thankfully he never would. Vince would refuse the job if offered, leave town and the nightmare would be over.

Devante drove her to the medical institute. Just thirty short minutes later, Dr. Allen had removed the cast, X-rayed her ankle and given a positive update. The bone was healing quickly and correctly. He didn't want her to put too much pressure on it yet and had given her an Aircast to keep it protected. But he'd given her the green light on driving. Next stop, rental car company.

She chose a black Hyundai Sonata. Sleek. Sporty. And undoubtedly less expensive than any car Julian would have chosen for her. After assuring Devante that she'd be fine, she plugged an address into the GPS, stopped at a drivethrough for a shake—and to put distance between her and Devante—and then headed back to Paradise Cove. It seemed she got there in no time. She pulled into the strip mall parking lot where she'd suggested they meet. It was nearing lunchtime, the parking lot fairly full. She parked on the back side of the mall, near an insurance company without much traffic. Less chances of being seen by any of the town's busybodies. Which Nicki had learned in a small town meant just about everybody.

Ten minutes passed. She was early. No big deal. Ten more minutes. A little late, but no need to panic. Or was there? Nicki had assumed Vince would be driving a rental. But what if someone from the community center picked him up? She sent a quick text, asking what kind of car he was driving and whether or not he was on his way. She also described her Sonata and where she was parked. Thirty harrowing minutes later, a late-model car whipped into the lot. She honked her horn. He spotted her and parked in the empty space next to her car.

Vince got out of the car, or more like uncoiled six

feet and five inches of strong bones and chiseled muscle from inside the low-key sedan she'd insisted upon when a sporty convertible or luxury model was what he would have rented. The whole point of being in PC was to hide, she'd reminded him. To be on the down low. To blend in.

She watched his slow, easy gait as he walked to her car. He could have driven a Ford truck like Julian's brother Warren and the rest of the ranchers. But he still would have stuck out like a rooster in a coop of guinea fowl as soon as he smiled. The same pearly whites that were on display as he opened her car door and sank into the seat beside her. The same boyish grin that separated women from their panties. That had caused Nicki to ignore her head's knowledge and her gut's warning against such and give the guy her number.

"Hey, beautiful."

His attempt at a kiss was stopped by a strong hand on a hard chest.

"Don't."

"What?" Vince asked, hands raised in mock innocence. "I was just going for your cheek, a friendly kiss."

"I'm not here to be friendly. I'm here to try to settle this craziness so you can get out of my life."

"Wow…"

"It's not personal, Vince. And that probably didn't come out the way that it should. This is a small town. That's the reason. And the Drakes are very much a part of it."

"Hell, looks like they own it."

"I came here to start a life with the man I love very much, who I've been with for years. And for you to follow me—"

"It's a free country. I need a job. Saw one that fit me. Applied. Simple as that."

"Not that simple, and you know it." Nicki reached for

her bag in the back seat and pulled out a sheet of paper. "I have the money—ten thousand, as promised. There will be two more payments of five thousand each. To have proof of this agreement, I've had what we agreed on put in writing. Not a lot of legal jargon. Quite concise. You agree to cease all contact with me following the receipt of this first payment. You also agree not to take the job at the community center and not to remain in Paradise Cove. We can wish each other the best and go our separate ways. I admit I really dislike being in this situation, but I don't hate you. There were some fun moments in that brief time we spent together. I'll choose to remember them." She held out the piece of paper and dug for a pen. It wasn't until she found one that she looked back up and realized Vince hadn't reached out for the paper she held.

"You've got to sign the agreement, Vince. I can't give you the money without it."

Vince huffed, looked over at her with narrowed eyes. "What if I said I don't want the money? What if I said it's too late for that?" He craned his neck from left to right and looked behind him. "I've never lived in a small town before. Looks like this one might grow on me."

"Vince, don't…"

He snatched the paper, folded in half. "Give me a day to think about it. Meet with Terrell. Then I'll decide what I'll do."

He opened the door.

"Vince, wait!"

"I've been waiting. It's your turn now."

Nicki sat stunned. What just happened? Away from the city, closeted in a small town, her bullshit radar had clearly quit working. Vince's flip of the switch caught her totally off guard. But she was no fool. Clarity came quickly. That asshole had never intended to settle this drama. He wanted to throw his *hell no* in her face. That in itself was bad enough, but life could get worse. He could be on his way to the center right now, ready to spill the beans about dating her to the first Drake who'd listen. Nicki started the car and tapped Julian's number seconds later. The music playing right now might be a treacherous dirge, but it was time to face it.

"Hey, baby."

Julian sounded so happy to hear from her. It hurt to know the joy wouldn't last long. "Hi. Are you busy?"

"Not right now. Just waiting to hear about your trip to the doctor, and how it feels to once again walk on two feet."

"It feels amazing."

"Really? You don't sound too happy."

"Actually, I'm not. We need to talk."

"What's going on?"

"I don't want to discuss it over the phone. Can I come by the office?"

"My next client arrives in about twenty minutes. How far are you from the office?"

"I'm back in town, so not that far. But I don't want to have this conversation in a rushed atmosphere."

"You're worrying me, Nicki. What's this about? Second thoughts on the AD position?"

"No, I'm really excited about developing that program."

"What then? Did you wreck the car?"

"No."

"Rob a bank?"

She smiled. "No."

"Then what? Listen, never mind. This is my last patient until after lunch. Why don't I head home afterward and we can talk there?"

"Okay. But just don't..." How would it sound for her to ask that he not talk to his brother? Not good. Really bad, in fact. "Never mind. I'll pick us up something for lunch. See you then."

The weather turned gloomy as quickly as Nicki's day. She hadn't known there was rain in the forecast. Didn't know bullshit was scheduled, either. A day full of surprises.

Since the weather had turned chilly, she decided on soup. Stopped by Julian's favorite deli and found that a lot of other residents had the same idea. She pulled up in front of the town house thirty minutes later. Felt she'd been inside only moments before hearing Julian's car. Busying herself with gathering dishes and reheating the soup, her back was to Julian when he entered the room. As if not looking at him would delay the inevitable. It did not.

"All right, Nicki. Tell me what's going on."

She turned. "Oh, hi, babe. Don't you want to sit down first? I just need to nuke the—"

"No, that can wait. The only thing I want right now is an explanation."

"Okay, but I might as well warn you. This won't be easy for me to say or for you to hear. It's about that guy who's been bugging me, trying to extort money." She paused for a response or a reaction. There was none. "It was Vince Edwards."

The merest crease appeared on his brow, but his voice was calm. "The ballplayer?" Nicki nodded. "The one coming in town to interview at the center? You two dated?"

"Briefly. Barely a month, as I told you before. Before you and I got back together, I had already found out what a jerk he was and had broken things off. Hadn't heard from him since ending it with him two years ago, until just before the show started on Broadway. Obviously he found out I was in it, made up a lie about me owing him and started the harassment."

"Why you, though? A guy like him has probably dated hundreds of women."

"I've asked myself that question a thousand times, almost every time I've had the misfortune to answer his call. I wouldn't knowingly. But a few times, especially around when the show was just getting started, I answered unknown and private numbers. That's how this started."

"When you say the two of you dated, did you sleep with him?"

Nicki nodded, answered softly. "Yes."

"Why didn't you tell me this before?"

"Because I know how you feel about that. Besides, I told you he and I dated."

"You told me you dated, but you didn't tell me you *dated*." He put a sarcastic emphasis on the last word. "You tried to make it sound casual, as in went to the movies or out to eat. Not like something that was intimate, the two of you connecting by having sex."

"Trust me, there was no connection—"

"There's always a connection." His tone was emphatic, but his voice did not rise. "Despite what society says, there is no such thing as casual sex. We were barely broken up a month, Nicki. How'd it happen?"

"I don't even know. Angry. Stupid. A rebound reaction, and one of the worst mistakes I've ever made." She looked directly at him for the first time, her eyes shiny with unshed tears. "It was only after finding out the truth about him and what a jerk he was that I felt truly ashamed for being an easy target, one of hundreds of women, as you said, who'd ignored the signs and drank the Kool-Aid."

"Yet he's not in any of their towns trying to get hired on where they've just taken a job. He's here. With a scheduled interview at the center that bears my name. And I'm just now finding out. That's messed up."

"I never thought the harassment would go this far. Thought him saying he'd come here was just a threat."

"Wait, he told you about coming here? When?"

"The day of the brunch. He sent a text."

"So you knew before I did. Before Terrell. You knew he was coming here and kept me in the dark!"

"I thought it was just a threat to get me to pay him. So I agreed to give him money. I didn't want you to know. He promised that afterward he'd leave me alone. But he lied."

"When did you last talk to him?"

"Today. I met with him to—"

Julian held up a hand. "You met with him? Here, in Paradise Cove?"

"In the strip mall parking lot to give him the money. But to get it he had to sign an agreement that put his promise to leave me alone in writing."

Julian leaned against the island. Was silent for a very long time. The silence made Nicki feel horrible. Then he started talking, and she felt even worse.

"Before I was confused, but now everything makes sense. The distractedness. The distance. You being nervous and jumpy and preoccupied. Sleeping with me every night while keeping secret communications with another man."

"Julian, it wasn't like that—"

"I asked you what was going on. Not once. Several times. On any one of those occasions, you could have trusted me, confided in me, but you didn't. You let my family entertain the notion of hiring your extortionist as a mentor to young children."

"Baby…"

He shook his head. "Don't. Not now. When I needed you to talk, when there should have been conversation, you were silent. But knowing I might find out the truth, you decide you want to bare all and tell me everything. Well, guess what. It's too late. I don't want to listen. Not to another word that you have to say."

Except for a word here or there, Julian never raised his voice. He turned and walked out of the house. Seconds later she heard the car leave the driveway.

When she went to bed, he still hadn't come home. Wasn't there when she awoke the next morning. There wasn't a word for how bad Nicki felt. Everything Julian had said was correct. There was no good excuse for why she hadn't told him everything from the beginning. That she hadn't had caused a horrible ending. The worst part about it was that she couldn't even put the fault for what had happened all on Vince. The person mostly to blame was herself.

Chapter 25

Before he'd only had a clinical perspective. But at this moment Julian knew from personal experience how a person could snap. He hadn't even known he could get this angry, let alone having ever experienced it before. As angry, hurt and disappointed as he was in Nicki, it was the dog Vince Edwards at the pit of his rage. He'd disrespected Julian's woman. Misled his family. No one mistreated his family like that and got away with it. Not on Julian Drake's watch.

He tapped the steering wheel and called his office. Cited an emergency and canceled his next appointment. Then he called Terrell.

"What's going on?"

"I need your face not to show what your ears are hearing."

A short pause. "Okay." The teasing quality had totally left Terrell's voice.

"Is Vince Edwards scheduled for an interview today?"

"Yeah, he'll be here in about an hour. Hold on a minute." Julian heard a series of noises, imagined his brother closing the door. "Okay, man, talk to me. No one can hear us. What's going on?"

"Something you're not going to believe." Julian took a deep breath, forced himself to stay calm as he relayed an abbreviated version of what he'd found out from Nicki. "She tried to explain, but I'd heard enough," he finished. "I thought nothing could hurt like her rejecting my proposal. But this type of betrayal? It's on another level. If you don't have trust, you don't have a relationship."

"It's a rare moment when I'm speechless," Terrell said

solemnly. "But I've got to tell you, bro. This is one of those times."

"Hard to find words for this situation. I finally get what I've always wanted—Nicki living here in Paradise Cove—then find out that a dude she slept with has followed her here, and some twisted game has been playing out the whole time that she's been with me. And the only reason she tells me is because he might mention it to you? That's a wrap, man. Done deal. It's over."

"Where are you headed now?"

"Your office, for the interview. I'm almost there. I've got a few questions to ask Vince Edwards. See what kind of threats he has to offer up when facing a real man."

Julian pulled into the parking lot a short time later and saw Jennifer's car. He wasn't surprised. The intensity with which he'd relayed the story about Nicki had probably frightened his brother into calling backup. The mere thought calmed Julian. A little.

A quick knock and he opened the door to Terrell's office. He and Jennifer were sitting at a small conference table. Warren was there, too. After hugging his mom and fist-bumping Terrell, he placed a hand on Warren's shoulder. "How'd they get you away from Charli? Tell you there was an angry bull loose that you might need to rope?"

"More like a coyote threatening the livestock that might need to be shot."

"Warren," Jennifer admonished, "do not say something like that, even in jest."

"Sorry, Mom."

Julian plopped into a nearby chair. "Guess y'all have already gotten the 411."

"Terrell told us what he knew," Jennifer answered. "But there's got to be more to the story."

"How do you figure?"

"Because I believe I know Nicki," Jennifer answered calmly. "She doesn't strike me as a cheater. Or a schemer who'd act with duplicitous motives."

"An hour ago I would have said the same thing. But the Nicki you know did all of that, right under my nose."

"I heard, son, and that's horrible. There is no denying or excusing the fact that she should have told you everything immediately. Up front. But I don't think she acted maliciously. You're angry and can't see it now. But from an objective stance, there is room for other perspectives. Don't get defensive," she hurriedly added. "I'm on your side. I just caution you to not be too hasty. To get the whole story, hear all angles, before making up your mind."

Jennifer left for a meeting. The brothers were mostly quietly waiting, until Terrell received the call that his appointment had arrived.

"You cool?" Terrell asked Julian.

"I'll make it a clean kick," Julian answered, referring to skills he'd honed for years as a black belt in martial arts.

"You heard what Mom said," Warren chided. "Don't joke like that."

"He's not joking," Terrell said, real concern on his face.

"I have no plans to get physical," Julian said finally. "If he has any sense at all, he won't say the wrong thing and have to get punched in the throat."

"Keep an eye on him," Terrell told Warren as he reached for the phone.

"Hello, Beatrice. Will you escort our visitor back to my office? Thank you."

A murmur of voices followed by laughter preceded a short knock on the door. A new, obviously besotted assistant announced Vince, who strolled into the office as though he owned the world. The door closed behind him.

He walked toward Terrell, now seated behind his desk, with hand outstretched. "Mr. Drake!"

Terrell didn't stand and barely smiled. "Have a seat, Vince."

The rude behavior was obviously unsettling. Even more so when Warren stood and walked toward the door and Vince realized he and Terrell were not alone. He looked at Julian, then back at Warren, now standing in front of the door as if to guard it.

Vince's smile dimmed as he sat. "I didn't realize this was going to be a group interview."

"There's a few things we didn't realize, either, my man." Terrell's tone was not unfriendly. "A situation involving my brother Julian—" he nodded toward the conference table where Julian now rested a hip "—and a person very important to him named Nicki Long. We need you to clear up a few things."

"And then we'll need you to get the hell out of this town," Julian said as he slowly walked over. "And not contact Nicki again."

Vince sat up straight in the chair. "Careful, brother. That sounds like a threat."

Julian offered a smile that didn't reach his eyes. "Oh no, Vince, only cowards do that. Real men like the Drakes don't make threats. We make promises. And we keep them. Harass Nicki again and you'll find out."

Thirty minutes later, Vince returned to his rental not quite sure how three men, talking calmly and smiling, put more fear in him than the punks he owed money had done while armed with guns. He'd never admit it. Was already creating an alternative truth in his head of why he decided not to work at the center. As for that witch Nicki, she wasn't worth him getting in any trouble. Especially here, in a town where he didn't know anybody and the Drakes were influential. Get arrested and there was no telling what would happen to him in jail. Vince would leave, but he'd remember the way he'd been treated. He'd come back here one day and bring his boys, the ones with records who were violent for real. Then he'd see how cool those Drake fools acted. Private school sissies raised on trust fund milk. He'd come back with backup, and even the score.

He checked the internet then plugged an address into his GPS. Minutes later he pulled into the parking lot of what seemed to be the town's lone restaurant. "Rinky-dink Hicksville," he muttered, anger increasingly replacing fear the farther he got from the center. "About all punks like those Drakes can handle."

He stepped inside and was surprised at the classy decor. There were only a few patrons. Not surprising, since it was almost two o'clock and most lunch hours had ended. There was no one at the host station, so Vince walked over to the bar and grabbed a seat. Pulled out his phone to check messages. The bartender was on the other side of the L-shaped counter, his back to Vince as he chatted with an attractive woman typing on a laptop. The woman looked up, made eye contact and smiled. A few seconds later, the bartender turned and walked over.

"Sorry about the wait, sir. What can I get you?"

Vince answered without looking up from his phone. "Rémy Martin, neat, and a glass of seltzer."

"Vince Edwards?"

Vince looked at the bartender, a handsome blond kid who didn't look old enough to serve liquor.

"Yeah, that's me."

"Man, I thought so! Dude! What are you doing here? I mean, it's cool and all. Of course, you can be anywhere you want. I'm just shocked. Sorry, my bad for rambling. Just a huge fan."

Vince's smile was slow and easy. The kid's excitement helped cover the negative feelings brought on by the Drakes questioning his manhood. Now he was being treated the way he was used to—as the superstar he was.

"What's your name, kid?"

"Jake." He held out his hand.

Vince shook it. "Nice meeting you, Jake. You sure you're old enough to work the bar?"

"Ah, man. I get that all the time. When I'm out socializing, I walk up to the bar with driver's license in hand."

"Ha!"

"Because I already know the drill. Vince Edwards! My buddies aren't going to believe this. Hey, mind if I get a selfie?"

"I'll think about it while I sip my drink."

"Oh, right. Drink. Sorry. Coming right up."

The bartender left to fix his drink. Vince watched him for a sec, then glanced over at the pretty lady. She was looking at him and, when caught, didn't immediately avert her eyes. Didn't walk over, either. Didn't matter. Vince knew the way he had with women. Knew she was trying to play hard to get. Another time and he might have joined her in the game. But he had business to handle. First, coming up with a way to get those fools their money. Then dealing with Nicki's boyfriend and his brothers.

"Here you go, sir, on the house."

Vince toasted with the snifter. "Appreciate it." He knocked it back in two gulps, gritted his teeth against the slow burn as the cognac trickled down his throat and chased it with the seltzer water. Checked out Jake talking with the woman again. Telling her a star was in the building. He was sure of that.

"Let me get another one, Jake. And a menu."

"Sure, right away." Jake brought over a menu.

"Make it a double this time."

"You got it."

Vince picked up the menu and leaned back against the bar seat. Soon there was movement in his peripheral vision. He knew that chick wouldn't be able to ignore his presence. Women never could.

Her floral-smelling cologne arrived before she did. "Bad day?"

He took his time looking up from the menu. "How do you figure?"

"Double shot at two in the afternoon. Mind if I sit here?"

He shrugged. "Chair's empty."

She perched on the seat, revealing a backside worthy of his attention. Pretty girl. A barracuda. He'd seen her kind time and again. He wasn't interested, but he wouldn't ignore her. He was a gentleman, after all.

"Anything worth ordering on this menu?"

"Best choice is the rib eye, medium rare." She opened her laptop and began typing.

Vince watched her fingers fly across the keys. "You must be a writer."

The woman smiled and revealed perfect white teeth and a dimple. Vince loved dimples. "A blogger. Why?"

"You type fast."

She nodded. "Jake says you're a basketball player from the East Coast."

"That why you came over? To blog about me?"

She stopped typing. "Not necessarily. I blog about celebrities. Jake knows you but I don't, so…" Her turn to shrug.

"That can easily be rectified." Vince held out his hand and flashed his panty-dropping smile. "Vince Edwards."

She countered with a look that Vince was sure had separated men from their money. "Ashley DeWitt."

"Nice to meet you, Ashley."

"Likewise."

"Now, since you know me, will I be in your blog?"

"Depends on what kind of juicy tidbits I can pry out of those tasty-looking lips. Do you have any?"

He thought briefly. Looked over and smiled. "I might. Are you familiar with the Drakes, the family that owns the community center?"

"Very familiar. I dated the mayor." Vince was obviously confused. "Ah, right. You're from out of town and might not know. Niko Drake is presently our town's mayor. But he looks poised to become the state's next senator."

"Is that so? What else can you tell me about them?"

"What would you like to know?"

Vince looked out at the near-empty dining room. "Why don't we discuss it over lunch? My treat. You might have information that could be beneficial to me, and I might give you a tip on a hot story."

Ashley slid off the stool with a hand on his thigh. "Follow me, Vince Edwards."

Vince picked up his drink and followed Ashley into the dining room. The Drakes wanted him gone by nightfall. But Vince might not be ready to leave so soon.

Chapter 26

Nicki sat in the middle of the master suite's walk-in closet, trying to squeeze way more clothes into a piece of luggage than it was designed to hold. It didn't seem as though she'd shopped that much since arriving, but the pile of clothes still needing to get packed told a different story. Was there time to run out and buy another suitcase? Maybe, but Nicki didn't want to stop to do that and have to come back. Somewhere between when she arrived and today, the town house had begun to feel like home, one she'd decorated. It was going to be hard enough to leave as it was. She only wanted to do it once.

She pulled out a stack of folded clothes and started to roll them, belatedly remembering that more clothes could get packed that way. Didn't surprise her that the thought hadn't come earlier. Considering how her whole world had been upended in the past forty-eight hours, she was amazed she could remember anything.

After thirty more minutes of trying the impossible, Nicki gave up on her single-piece-of-luggage concept. She'd place the extra items in a recyclable bag and buy another piece of luggage at the airport. There was plenty of time for her to catch the red-eye. But she needed time to go to the rental agency and have Devante added as a driver so that he could return the car after dropping her off at Oakland International. Thank God he'd given her his card that included a cell phone number. Aside from the Drakes, he was the only person in town that she knew. With any luck, she'd be able to depart without having to see the family.

A bit cowardly, she readily admitted. But easier. Necessary. It broke her heart to have hurt Julian the way she did.

The man was in pain. Evidenced by how he hadn't come back to the town house or returned her calls. After waking up to his empty side of the bed for the second day in a row, she got his silent message. There was nothing left between them to talk about. Her lies, no matter how well intended, had backfired and cost her the love of her life. It was over. Julian was done.

Feeling the onslaught of tears and refusing to shed any more, she jumped up and went into the bathroom for her toiletries. While gathering them she mentally went over the email she'd sent Jennifer. The one resigning from a position she hadn't started. Apologizing for any inconveniences caused by her departure. Admitting she hated to leave but knowing it was for the best. And the one she'd sent Julian, stating all of that and the depth of her love. After one last look around, she ran a finger across the smooth, cool marble countertop and headed downstairs for a recyclable bag. She reached the landing and was startled when the doorbell rang. Walked over, looked out the peephole and opened the door with a sigh.

"Mrs. Drake, hello."

"Nicki, we've come much too far to revert to formalities."

"You're right, I'm sorry. Just wasn't expecting anyone."

"It is how I intended. Wasn't sure that had I asked you would have agreed to the visit. May I come in?"

"Sure." She stepped back so that Jennifer could enter. "Can I get you something? Water or tea?"

"Tea sounds lovely, dear. Chamomile if you have it."

Nicki went into the kitchen, grateful for the chance to get over the shock of Jennifer showing up at the front door. Time to put on her grown-girl girdle and take the verbal lashing Julian's mother had undoubtedly come to deliver. After setting the kettle to boil, she joined Jennifer on the sofa.

"The water will be ready in a few minutes."

"Good." An awkward silence followed as Jennifer eyed Nicki thoughtfully. "I must admit, your email came as quite a surprise."

"This week has been full of them."

"More for some than others, I'm told."

"Whatever it was that Julian told you, know that every story has two sides."

"That is correct. The story told from his point of view is quite damning. I'd like to hear yours."

The kettle whistled. Nicki prepared the drinks and carried the mugs back into the living room.

She took a sip and a breath. "I love Julian very much and would never set out to purposely hurt him. Whatever you think of what I'm about to share with you, please know that, Jennifer. Your son is the love of my life.

"In the twenty-twenty vision of hindsight, it's clear that I should have told him everything up front. I didn't lie, not outright. I just didn't tell him everything at once. I told him I'd dated someone while he and I were broken up. He didn't ask for a name, and I didn't offer one. He didn't ask whether or not we'd slept together, and I thought it best not to share that, either. It was a fling borne out of the hurt from the breakup. And it was over. So why tell him about it? We were back together, and for me, that's all that mattered."

Nicki continued to pour out her heart. Jennifer sipped tea and listened.

"With everything that's happened," she finished, "I knew there was no longer a place for me at the center or in this town. Julian doesn't want to be around me. His actions have made that very clear. So I felt it best to leave quickly, quietly. Go back home and begin to pick up the pieces of my life."

"I appreciate your honesty, Nicki. Thank you for sharing

your side. Out of all of my sons, Julian is easily the smartest
and the most sensitive. You're right. He is deeply hurt by
your betrayal, especially since it happened while the two
of you were in such close proximity, and because it went
on for so long. It seems clear that had you the opportunity
for a do-over, you'd handle the situation differently. But…"

Jennifer paused as her phone chimed. She reached inside her designer bag and pulled it out. "It's Julian. One
moment." She tapped the screen. "Hello, son." A pause to
listen. "Actually, I'm at your house, talking with Nicki."
She glanced at Nicki, her brow slightly creased. "What?
When? Hold on a moment. Nicki, can you turn on the tele-
vision to local news?"

Nicki opened a compartment of the coffee table, pulled
out the remote and tapped the power button. Then she
changed the channel to the local station, where a banner
along the bottom of the screen announced breaking news.
"We've got it, son. Let me call you back."

Just as Jennifer ended the call, a picture of Vince came
on the screen.

Nicki turned up the volume.

"Edwards claims the original dispute was between him
and ex-girlfriend Nicki Long."

"What?"

"…a professional dancer most recently seen in the hit
Broadway musical *A Hair's Tale*, now dating local resident
Dr. Julian Drake. According to the former basketball star,
the Drakes lured him to Paradise Cove under the false pre-
tense of potential employment and then allegedly proceeded
to threaten his life. Edwards says they backed down when
he vowed to take the dispute public and was then offered
money by Long to stay quiet and leave town."

"Oh my God!" Nicki jumped up from the couch. "He's
such a liar!"

The TV cut to a location shot of Vince. "I was shocked," he said, looking at the reporter who was offscreen. "I was excited about the chance to mentor the type of boys who grew up like I did. And to be blindsided like that, when expecting an interview? And then this bribery attempt?" He held up the paper that Nicki had given him. She wanted to throw up. "From everything I'd read, the Drakes are an upstanding family. But behind the suits and professional facade, they're just a bunch of thugs."

"What do you plan to do, Mr. Edwards?" the reporter asked.

"I'm not going to do anything," Vince said with a smile. "I have an attorney to fight those kinds of battles. They'll be hearing from him very soon."

"Just when I thought he couldn't sink lower..." Her voice trailed off as Nicki seethed.

"For some there is no limit to the depths they'll go when money is involved."

"Right. Money he was trying to get from me, which is why he badgered me and why I finally agreed to paid him. Not that crap he just spouted on TV."

"Of course, but the truth wouldn't warrant a lawsuit." Jennifer appeared unmoved, her countenance almost one of boredom.

Nicki grabbed her phone. "What's the name of that station, Jennifer? Their call letters. Do you know?"

"Stay calm, Nicki. This isn't the first time we've danced with a frivolous lawsuit, which is certainly coming."

"I still need to contact them and set the record straight."

"What are you going to do?"

"I'm going to go down there and tell the truth about what happened. I will not let him tarnish Julian's name. Or the Drakes'."

Jennifer appraised Nicki with a spark in her eye. "Spoken with such conviction, one would mistake you for a Drake yourself."

"I'm afraid I've ruined those chances."

"Maybe. Maybe not. But one thing's for sure. You're not going to help the situation by running away."

"I'm not running away."

"That's exactly what you're doing."

"I'm leaving a place where I'm no longer wanted."

"You're leaving a man who is angry and hurt, and rightfully so. But as you said, there are two sides to every story, at least. As a woman, I understand yours. Brief fling. Over and done with. Forget about it. Move on. It makes sense that you wouldn't tell Julian. But once the threats continued, and you knew Vince was on his way here…"

"I used the advance to try to stop him. It was money, not me that he wanted. Vince promised me if I gave him the money, he wouldn't take the job at the center and he'd leave me alone for good. Knowing the kind of man he is, I couldn't give him the money without proof of that promise. That's why I wrote the agreement. I thought the problem had been handled. That's why I didn't tell Julian. It's too late for all that now. He doesn't want to talk to me—he hasn't come home for two nights straight."

"He's at our home, honey, and he hasn't wanted to talk to me, either. He's an introspective man who needs time alone with his thoughts. Space to ponder and work out his feelings. I can tell you this much—he doesn't want you to leave."

"Humph. I can't tell."

"If my son is truly the love of your life, as you claim, leaving now, with things as they are, would be the worst possible move. Drake men are some of the strongest, proudest, most stubborn, confident—some would say arrogant— men I've ever known. Yet if one is fortunate enough to win their heart, no man will love you stronger or better. This, I know for sure.

"He doesn't want you to leave, Nicki, and quite frankly I don't, either. Nor do I want to force you to stay—which, technically and legally, since you've already signed the contract to work at the center, I could do. I will say that the timing is especially unfortunate given an exceptional opportunity I'd planned to share with you before…everything happened. One that I feel could have provided quite a boost in your professional career. Some might even have called it a chance of a lifetime. Not to mention a rather hefty paycheck. But never mind."

"What is it?"

Jennifer hesitated. "I'm really not sure I should tell you, Nicki. Given your plans to return to New York."

"That's a wicked smile, Mrs. Drake. I think you absolutely should tell me."

"Oh, well. If you insist. It involves a director named Ngo Xhe. Have you heard of him?"

"I've met him. Julian and I saw his show in LA. It's fantastic!"

"So I've heard. One of my well-connected friends, a patron of the arts, is among several helping to sponsor a USA tour, performing in several major cities. I mentioned how wonderful it would be if he could put on some kind of show at the center, a fund-raiser during the holidays or the first part of next year. She wasn't sure he could actually do the show himself but thought he might be able to lend us some dancers. All of this would require coordination and expertise, of course, but considering the level of people who support our endeavors, the rewards through connections made and the networking possible could be quite significant. Dear, what time is your plane?"

Nicki canceled her flight. She called the network and

scheduled an interview while Jennifer fielded calls from family and friends. It hadn't taken long for everyone in town to know what happened. Those who hadn't seen the report on TV had found it online. By six o'clock the story had broken nationally. By the time Jennifer left an hour later, the Drakes' lawyers had been called to handle Vince, and the two women had hashed out plans for a Valentine's weekend fund-raising gala. That was less than four months away. The day had proved emotionally exhausting, yet Nicki was glad it had happened, and awed at how differently problems could be handled when one had power and money. If she'd shared everything with Julian the moment Vince's threats started, the problem would have ended a long time ago.

Nicki went upstairs to unpack the suitcase. Happy that she was staying in town and excited about her professional future. Her ankle was almost healed, she'd soon be back dancing, and without so much as a phone call let alone an audition, she was set to choreograph a holiday show with Ngo Xhe's dancers! Would she and Julian get back together? Only time would tell. Was the saga with Vince finally over? She certainly hoped so. But for now, and the next four months at least, she'd be too busy to worry.

Chapter 27

Julian felt he'd lived four lives in less than a month. So much had happened. Everything had changed. The rift with Nicki. Vince showing up in PC. The all-hands-on-deck push for his brother during the final week of campaigning. An endless round of parties after Niko won. All this while still handling a full roster of patients. Counseling other people while feeling *he* needed therapy. Or a vacation, at the very least. Instead he sat in Niko's office having just agreed to take on more work.

"I know you've got a lot on your plate, Doctor, so I really appreciate you agreeing to serve as a consultant."

"I'm still trying to figure out how you got me to do it. I came here totally prepared to say no—had a list of valid reasons and everything."

Niko chuckled. "Power of persuasion. Can't be a successful attorney without the ability to present a compelling argument. Plus, I know how passionate you are about the problems facing the health-care system. As the most populous state in the nation, I feel an even greater need to make sure the proper plans remain in place for agencies such as Medicare and Medicaid, no matter what's happening in Washington. Because of our large immigrant population, we have a lot of little ones who need access to preventative services and the area on which you're most focused, mental health."

"I must admit that's the driving factor in my decision to be a part of the Committee on Health. To be able to help contribute to bills that will decrease America's dependence on prescription medication. To expand the definition of post-traumatic stress beyond military personnel to one that includes average citizens growing up in American neighborhoods with worse violence than those in the Middle East is an opportunity I couldn't turn down."

"Being part of the solution."

"Exactly."

"Speaking of solutions, what's going on with you and your lady?"

"Nothing much."

"You haven't talked to her?"

"Not really."

"Why not?"

"She's been out of town. Went to LA right after the election. Was there a couple weeks working on the dance. After that she went back east to sublet her place and spend Thanksgiving with her mom."

"Her phone doesn't work outside PC?"

"We talked a few times, but there's a lot going on. Especially with her back working, choreographing the show…"

Niko eyed him intently. Julian fought the urge to squirm under his older brother's intent gaze. Like Julian, Niko was keenly intuitive and paid as much attention to what someone didn't say as what they did.

"So y'all haven't talked because she's working?"

"We've both been busy. On top of my usual workload, I've been back and forth to San Diego, fulfilling a promise I made to Dexter's wife Faye about counseling teens who'd been treated at her clinic. And I've been helping the state's new senator."

"Ah, no. Don't put any of that on me, bro. I'm never too busy to talk to Monique. My wife and I talk every single day. No matter what. No matter where. What about the ballplayer? He still in PC?"

"No, he left."

Julian purposely left out details on that exit, the persuasion used to ensure that Edwards left town. Terrell had refused to provide specifics regarding what happened. All Julian knew was that the solution had involved one of Ace's contacts from his old neighborhood in Oakland—someone whose background matched that of Nicki's nemesis. Someone who spoke a street language Vince understood.

"I don't know the whole story. It's not my business at all. But what I do know is how happy you were when you were dating Nicki. How in love the two of you appeared not long ago in New York, and here. Is what happened between her and that guy so egregious you can't get past it?" Julian shrugged. "I don't think so. Because if what happened had been a deal breaker, the two of you would have officially broken up by now."

"It's about a betrayal of trust. Of lies and deception. I love Nicki, no doubt. Wanted to spend the rest of my life with her. All she needed to do was tell me what was going on. Tell me the truth. Why did she lie? That remains a question in my mind."

"Have you asked her?"

"Of course."

"And…"

"The guy was extorting her. She didn't want me to know. Knew I'd handle the situation but was concerned about how I'd handle it."

"I can kind of understand that, brother. You know what they say. Gotta watch those quiet ones. Plus, you are a third-degree black belt. Sounds like her actions were to protect you."

"I'm sure that's the way it plays in her mind. For me, though, what most stands out is the broken trust. I don't know if I can get past that. Or if it's something I can live with."

"Only you know that, bro. But ask yourself this. Is Nicki the kind of woman you can live without?"

Julian's ringing cell phone broke the silence. He pulled it from his pocket. "My assistant," he explained. "Yes, Katie."

He paused, listened, watched Niko begin to check his phone. "Excuse me, what? Dr. Johnson?"

Upon hearing that name, Niko looked up.

"Where'd you hear this?" Julian leaned against the chair back, his face a mask of concern. "No, I appreciate you calling. Both of them? All right, Katie. Anything else?" He listened, nodded. "Right. No, I'll be heading home shortly, just waiting for rush hour to die down a bit, and in the office first thing in the morning." Julian continued to listen. "Put it in my inbox. I'll take a look at it. Okay. See you then."

He ended the call, stared into space.

"What's going on, man?"

"Something crazy."

"I heard the name Johnson. He get busted again?"

"No, his daughter Natalie just got arrested. She got pulled over for speeding. The police searched her car. Found a large stash of prescription drugs. Threw on the cuffs." A pause and then, "She wasn't alone. Ashley was with her and got arrested, too."

"I didn't know even know they were friends! So instead of the doctor, his daughter was dealing pills?"

"Possession of a controlled substance with intent to distribute is how they were charged. Is there evidence to prove it?" Julian shrugged. "I knew they were very close and believe Natalie used that friendship and Ashley's blog to come against me. The doctor wasn't charged, but announced his immediate retirement."

"Brother, your business is going to boom."

"Doesn't feel good making money on someone else's misfortune."

"Someone has got to service those clients. It might as well be you."

"At least now Natalie's actions make more sense. The fewer patients her dad had on his books, the fewer medications it would appear he needed, and if she was stealing inventory...wow, that's really too bad. Ironic that I get this news while in your office. This kind of drug proliferation is the very reason why I agreed to be a consultant for the Committee on Health. We've got to do something about prescription-drug abuse."

"That's why I asked you to come on board, bro. You are the man for the job."

Julian looked at his watch and stood. Niko did, too. "Heading out?"

"I think traffic's lightened up enough to make it a quick drive. Are you getting a place here? Commuting? How does that work?"

"Monique and I have talked about getting either condos or townhomes both here and in DC. I'll actually spend more time in Washington than I will here in Sacramento, which of course is fine with Monique. She has friends and colleagues on the East Coast and will likely travel with me on those occasions. It's a new chapter in our lives, one that we're going to write together."

"I always saw you two as the family's power couple."

"That title would probably go to London and Ace."

"They'd definitely get the paparazzi couple award."

Niko chuckled. "Yes, and our baby sister loves every minute of it."

The two men hugged. Julian walked toward the door.

"Ju."

He turned around.

"Call Nicki. Talk to her. Work it out."

"I hear you."

"Don't go with your head on this, bro. Go with your heart."

It was just over seventy miles from Sacramento to Paradise Cove. Julian spent sixty-five of them thinking about Nicki, Niko's instruction to call her and, even more, his question about living a life without her. In many ways it was as though his life officially began only after she'd come into it. Could he live without her? Yes. It would be difficult, but there'd never been anything Julian couldn't accomplish when he put his mind to it. What really mattered was the question he now asked himself.

Did he want to?

Chapter 28

Nicki stood front and center in the Drake Community Center auditorium. She faced the stage, head high, arms raised with the focus of a conductor. Fifteen pairs of eyes were on her. Excited young teens who attended the center, talented and lucky enough to have been chosen to be a part of the Valentine-themed show's finale. Paige had flown over to help with rehearsals and because *A Hair's Tale* was on break could be in the show!

"Cue the music! Get ready, guys. One, two, three, four! Pow! Big movements. Smile. Turn. Pop. Two. Three. Four. Step. Step. Good!" She directed the dance with her body and soul. Shouting out counts. Steps. Encouraging them on. Joining in on the parts they'd all dance together. It was only the first two eight counts with several missteps, but considering these girls were not professional dancers, had only seen Ngo Xhe's show on tape and had only practiced the intricate dance steps for just over a week, they did well. Nicki didn't coddle them because they were beginners. She set high expectations and demanded their best. She assured them that excellence lived inside them. Helped them believe. In return they worked to prove her right. Over and over they practiced. Individually. In groups. And then back on stage. Finally, an hour later, she announced that practice was over.

She walked to the center of the stage. Paige joined her. "Gather round, guys." The teens and Nicki were joined by the ten professional dancers from Ngo's troupe at the heart of the ninety-minute program. The group formed a circle and grabbed hands.

"Okay, ladies, good job today. One of the things I want

everyone to focus on during tonight's visualization are the transitions from one formation to another. One line into two. Right now that's real sloppy. Understandable—it's only been a week and this is a new way of dancing. But it's important to remember that the steps, transformations, music all work together, so we need to see that happening in our minds. Then it becomes easier for our bodies to follow. Everyone understand?" She raised her hand as a sign for their answer. All around her hands shot up in the air.

"You all are visualizing, right? For five minutes before you go to sleep? Seeing the dance and you doing it perfectly?" Some teens responded audibly. Others nodded. "Well, a couple of you might want to add another five minutes, because clearly no practice outside here has been done. I'm not calling out any names—Carissa, Michelle, Angelique—I'm just saying…"

The group laughed along with her. "Those ladies know why they got pointed out, but we all can and will improve. That's why it's called practice. The more we practice, the more perfect we become. So have a great weekend, everybody. Get in a little rest and a lot of practice. Next week we'll add on the next set of eight counts to what was learned this week. Any questions?" She looked around the circle. "No? Then that's it. Good job, dancers."

The group of excited teens began to disperse. Several of them came up to hug Nicki. Others chatted or checked their phones as they left the auditorium.

Paige strolled over. "I love this type of dancing, Nicki. It's such fun!"

"Isn't it? I'm so glad you're here. Just wish you could stay the whole time."

"I wanted to, but with Mike a long stay was a no go."

"Problems?"

"No. But I'd promised him that my break from performing was to spend more time with him. Instead I'm here. With you."

"Performing," they said together.

"I'll watch the tapes and work on my dance. That and a week of rehearsals right before and I'll be ready to shine." Paige turned to leave. "You heading out?"

"No, think I'll work on my dance a little bit. What time is your flight?"

"First thing mañana. That's why I wanted a hotel close to the airport tonight."

"Devante will take good care of you." They hugged. "Love you, girl. Text me when you get home so I know you've arrived safely."

Once alone, Nicki sat and went through a series of stretches, then walked over to the sound system. Soon a mellow, piano-driven jazz piece filled the air. It was the solo piece that would anchor the program's first half. The stage bare save for Nicki and a spotlight. She walked to a point on the stage just beyond the curtain, raised to her full height of five feet, eight inches, and assumed ballet's fourth position. She wore denim-inspired dance pants and a faded, cropped, long-sleeved tee emblazoned with the words *Live Your Life*. On the next downbeat, she took a step. Leg straight, toe pointed, then into a twirl. Her moves were fluid, flawless, her body an instrument of beauty as she executed a series of steps. Split leaps. Pirouettes. Elevating the basic steps of Xhe's original lulu when the song's tempo quickened into a midtempo beat. She felt herself get lost in the music and movements. In this moment, nothing existed but the dance. Worries took a back seat. Problems faded. She was one with the music.

The routine crescendoed and then eased back into the romantic melody from which it began. Her movements became graceful, sensuous, expressing the emotion of love with her body better than others could do with their voice. As the last notes faded, she floated to the ground and ended with legs stretched, back arched, arm touching the floor behind her. The song ended. She held the position, ignored her body's complaint at being contorted. Stayed until she heard a single clap.

Her eyes flew open as she sat up abruptly. Another clap happened. And another. And more. She looked out, unable to see past the first few rows.

"Tangie?"

It would make sense for the dancer from Ngo's company serving as her assistant to have stayed to watch her work on the dance. The claps increased as a person walked into view. It wasn't Tangie.

"Julian."

He continued clapping until he stood directly before her. "Girl, you were born to be a dancer. That was…magic."

"Thanks. It's a work in progress, but I like how it feels."

"I don't see how it can get any better."

"How long were you watching?"

"I saw it all."

Her voice was calm but her heartbeat skipped and jumped with excitement. Had she manifested this man on the strength of desire? Could he feel that he was the muse who'd inspired her movements? Did he know that it was her love for him at the heart of the dance?

"I like your top."

Nicki looked down, then back up with a smile. "It's one of my favorites."

"Our first official date."

"Prudential Center. Newark, 2011."

"Rihanna was all of that, man. And when that song started up and T.I. came on stage…madness."

"Pandemonium. Everybody went crazy! I still don't

know how you managed to keep the shirt hidden until the show was over and we were back in the car."

Julian nodded, said nothing. His eyes narrowed, thinking. Nicki wished she knew what about. For a time, mere seconds, they'd been back in the couple flow. Easy camaraderie. Julian had almost smiled. Then a return to uncomfortable silence.

"I've hardly seen you here lately."

"I've been back and forth to Sacramento doing work with my brother, and to Faye's clinic in San Diego."

A few seconds passed. Then a few more. Nicki tried to read his face. Julian looked beyond her to a space on the wall.

"Has he settled in yet?"

"Taking to it like a duck to water."

Nicki reached over for a towel and a bottle of water. She blotted the perspiration on her forehead, took a long, healthy swig.

"How was Thanksgiving with Miss Marie?"

"Unorthodox." Julian raised his brow. "Chinese food and a guided tour of the African American museum in DC."

"Nice. Just you two?"

Nicki shook her head. "There were about fifteen or twenty of us."

"Surprised they were open on a holiday."

"I was, too. While there I learned that Christmas is the only day that they're closed."

The small talk continued, punctuated by pauses. Unlike Nicki's dance it was stilted, unsure. She knew why. Hard to have a conversation around the elephant standing between them.

"Julian, can we sit and talk, really talk, for a minute?"

"Actually, I was on my way out. Just happened to hear the music and came to see what was happening."

"Just a few minutes. We've hardly seen each other in almost a month. Living here with us not talking is driving me crazy."

"You've barely been here."

"I'm here now. I know you needed space and time and all that. But I want to make sure you understand everything. And then after that…the next move will be on you."

"All right."

He turned and walked halfway up the auditorium. Beyond the stage lights and into the shadows. Nicki followed, and when he sat down she took the chair beside him, turned to face him as directly as possible and began to share her heart.

"I never imagined myself living here. You know that better than anybody. As much as I love you—and that's more than I've ever loved anyone—Broadway always stood between me and that possibility. Then life happened, and just like that I'm not only living here but working and dancing. But it still feels like a situation that's contrary to reason, because I'm living in your home and hometown without you. I've signed on as artistic director for a year. But honestly? If this is how it's going to be between us, I'll break the contract, because I simply can't deal.

"I understand why you got so upset. I get it now. I've apologized. I meant it. That's all I can do. I can't do it over. I can't take anything that happened back. If we could rewind time, I would definitely do things differently. It would have made my life easier. I see that now. Once you and your family found out about Vince, the issue was resolved. It was like, one and done. But at the time I made the decisions I did, it was for the right reasons. I thought he was someone I could handle—I had no idea he would take it as far as he did. Especially since what he said was a lie and I didn't owe him anything. But there's another reason. Something else I didn't tell you."

He'd been looking straight ahead, but at this revelation, Julian looked her in the eye.

"A week or so after he started calling, I got home and realized there was nothing to drink. So I hopped up and headed to the store. No problem, right? It wasn't that late, around eleven o'clock. On my way back, these two guys who'd parked in front of my house got out of their car. Didn't think much about it, but they had my attention. I am a New Yorker, after all."

Nicki's attempt to lighten the situation didn't work.

"We got to a place on the sidewalk at the same time. When I tried to go around them, they blocked my path. They knew who I was, said Vince had sent them to collect his money. Thank goodness for my nosy neighbor, Miss Frances. She hollered a greeting, and they let me by. That's when the situation became serious in my mind, and I felt threatened. A part of me wanted to tell you. Paige kept insisting that you needed to know. But I knew if that happened, you would have been on the very next flight and things would have definitely escalated. I couldn't have lived with being responsible if anything happened to you. It was a few days later that the accident happened and I came here. Situation over. Problem solved. End of story. Until it wasn't. The problem that I thought was over followed me here."

She placed her hand on top of his. "I'm sorry, baby. And I miss you. Can we work this out and get back together? I'm going crazy being alone in the town house. The nights are too quiet, and beyond the dancing I'm totally bored."

"Sounds like you don't want a man. You just want company."

"Pretty much."

For the first time since he'd walked in, Julian smiled.

"I appreciate you trusting me enough to share everything. It's probably better that I didn't know about it before. That you didn't share that until after he'd left town. But don't ever do it again, Nicki. You hear me?" She nodded. "Don't ever try to deal with something like that on your own. Protecting you is my responsibility. It's what a man does."

"I get that now."

"Good." He stood, stretched. "I'm headed out to get something to eat. Want to join me?"

She stood, too. "I would, except I have a conference call with my agent in thirty minutes. Just enough time to shower and have a quick bite. Maybe we can hang out tomorrow night?"

"Maybe."

Men and their pride, Nicki thought as they parted. He wanted to come back on his schedule, his timetable. Jennifer had encouraged her to exercise patience. She'd also said that a love worth having was worth fighting for.

Reaching for her phone, she sent Julian a quick text.

Want to come over later and massage my sore muscles?

She waited. No answer. Started up her car and headed home. A few minutes later, her phone pinged. Once stopped at a red light, she checked it.

A text back from Julian.

Yes. I have a muscle that needs rubbing, too.

Nicki laughed out loud. Turned on the stereo, turned the music up loud. Her baby was coming over. They were going to rub muscles and spend the night doing her favorite dance with the best partner ever.

Chapter 29

December and January had flown by in the blink of an eye. Nicki could hardly believe it was Valentine's Day weekend and the charity gala had finally arrived.

She peeked from behind the curtain to check out the crowd. San Francisco's War Memorial and Performing Arts Center was filled to capacity. When Jennifer told her she'd have no problem selling out three thousand seats, Nicki had her doubts—not only about the relatively short window to promote and sell tickets, but that it was five hundred dollars for the least expensive seat. But she'd done it. Not only would the Drake Community Center benefit, but so would Nicki, as part of the funds would be used for the arts program Nicki would run.

Less than six months ago, Nicki had had life all planned out, and it had looked nothing like the one she lived right now. Then, she'd been focused on back-to-back Broadway shows, saving money to build her portfolio, continuing a long-distance relationship with Julian and eventually talking him into moving his practice back east so that he could counsel, she could dance and they both could live happily ever after. Now, here she was about to lead a troupe of seasoned professionals and a few exceptionally talented Drake Community Center dancers in the lulu, Ngo Xhe's original dance.

Looking beyond the glittering gowns and starched tuxes that filled the orchestra level, Nicki spotted the Drake clan in their private box. Julian's parents sat in the middle of the first row, flanked by Ike Jr. and Quinn on their right and Niko and Monique to their left. Behind them sat Terrell and Aliyah, Teresa and London. Nicki guessed Ace and Atka were together, getting drinks or doing something equally mundane, like plotting a world takeover. Warren was home with the new baby. She didn't see Julian, who'd said that he'd come. They'd done well the past couple months. Just before the new year, he'd come back home. Had there been a flashback to the hurt she'd caused him? Had the news that Vince Edwards now coached at a high school near San Francisco made him doubt some or all of what she'd sworn was true? Nicki closed her mind against the onslaught of thoughts. There was time only for positive energy. She had a show to do.

Paige joined Nicki at the curtain, peeked over her shoulder. "Wow, it's crowded."

"Yep, a sold-out house."

"Not quite Broadway."

"It's even better." Nicki turned to Paige. "Never thought you'd hear me say that, huh?"

"Not in a million years. Not surprised, though. Love tends to wipe out the logical and accurate-thinking side of one's brain."

"And on that note…" Nicki gave a playful nudge as she walked past her. "Let's get dancing." She reached for Paige's hand, clasped it into her own. "And let's hope that in the very near future you lose your mind, too."

"I love you more than most, Nicki Long. But move to the West Coast? My honey would never."

"But you are going to audition for Ngo Xhe's next show, right? It's in San Francisco, but only twelve weeks."

"Definitely going to try out for that one. Mike can handle cross-country visits for that length of time."

"I'm so glad you're here."

"Me, too. And I'm happy for you. Love's got you glowing. Congratulations."

Backstage, the dancers gathered in a circle, waiting for

Nicki. She and Paige joined them, still holding hands, and clasped the hands of the dancers next to them. Nicki smiled at the professionals and took in the nervous, excited looks of the teens from the center.

"I was you once," she began, looking at her first crop of community center dancers. "Standing backstage at my very first professional show. Nervous, excited, not sure if I'd remember the steps. Petrified I'd mess up the entire routine." She paused and looked each girl in the eye. "You will remember. And if you don't, your body will. And if your body doesn't, it's still okay. Because your heart is in the right place. And so are you. Out there, on stage, even your mistakes will look like magic. Just keep smiling and flowing to the rhythm of the beat. Remember how absolutely beautiful, talented and amazing you are. Now, repeat after me.

"I am exceptional. I am amazing. I can do anything I want to do and be anything I want to be. Tonight, I am a dancer. Wait, I didn't hear you. Tonight, I am what?"

"A dancer!" the girls shouted, and the pros, too.

"That's right. We are dancers. Let's go out there and make the lulu come alive!"

Moments later the music began, pulsating percussion against a pitch-black stage. With a hidden light to guide them, the ten girls trained at the Drake Community Center danced across the stage—syncopated claps and stomps with their feet. Driving the movement. Creating the beat. The professional dancers entered next. Twirling and leaping, gliding and marching. Fluorescent red stripes on their black leotards came alive, as did more percussion instruments, then horns, then strings.

Three minutes into the first song, Nicki entered, a bundle of energy, a body of grace, combining years of training in modern dance with jazz, a little tap and a touch of ballet, mimicking the other dancers as they marched and then flawlessly inviting the audience to clap along and tap their feet in time to the contagious rhythm. During the first segment, the dancers introduced the story. About a group of girls, friends, outcasts all, who found their voices in their feet. On the final notes of the song preceding the first half's finale, dancers twirled and danced themselves off-stage, leaving the stage bare save Nicki and the spotlight.

She performed her solo dance. In her mind it was for Julian. Becoming one with the music, she poured her love for him from her heart to her limbs. Expressed the joy he brought her in every leap, her excitement in every spin. The music slowed and with it her movements. A series of dance moves took her to the back of the stage. In a final flurry of arms and legs in fluid motion, she returned to the center of the stage. As the last notes of the song played out, she was slowly lifted up from the floor. Higher and higher, until she disappeared into the rafters.

The unexpected move stunned the crowd, evidenced by their collective gasp. Seconds of silence passed, and then thunderous applause began. Nicki smiled as she hurried out of the harness that had lifted her safely to the ceiling's rafters and a narrow walkway to a ladder behind the back curtain. Her plan to end the first half on a high, showstopping note had worked better than she imagined. It would be topped only by her solo before the group finale, again the way she'd planned it. A cocoon for her students' first performance, and their inevitable faux pas. However they performed and whatever happened in between these well-polished acts would be forgotten. Nicki felt certain that the show would be labeled a success, both as a sold-out fundraiser and artistically, as a show she'd designed. A dancer and choreographer? Who knew!

With two forty-minute sets and a fifteen-minute intermission, the evening flew by. Sweaty and exhausted but pumped with adrenaline, Nicki smiled and preened and dazzled the audience, even as she mentally prepared for her heart-stopping finale. This would be the truest test yet of how well her ankle had healed.

"This is it, Nicki," she mouthed to herself while dancing over to the far side of the stage. "You can do it." Then, with a running start, she cartwheeled into a handless backflip over ten pairs of shoes. She heard another collective audience gasp as she landed on the other side, executed perfect piqué turns to the center of the stage and ended with a dramatic flourish of fingers as she dropped into a Chinese split.

The audience went wild. She stood, waved and exited the stage as each group of dancers took their bows. After Paige and the principal dancers were acknowledged, Nicki returned to the stage, the rousing standing ovation now minutes long. She clasped the hands of the dancers next to her as they took one final collective bow. As they did so, Nicki noticed Jennifer being ushered up the stairs to the stage. Turning, she applauded the woman who'd organized the night's performance.

Jennifer acknowledged the crowd, then pulled Nicki into a warm embrace. "Fabulous! Absolutely amazing," she whispered. "I'm so proud of you."

Then, taking the mike from an assistant who waited, she addressed the crowd, eyes twinkling. "I told you tonight's show would be worth every dollar. Was I right?"

The audience cheered their affirmative response.

"I want to thank everyone involved in helping to make tonight's event a huge success through supporting, promoting and making the arts available to all children and teens everywhere. To the Ladies of Paradise—the very active women's society of Paradise Cove—the businesses and corporations of Paradise Cove, San Francisco and surrounding communities, for your largesse in donations of both money and resources, to the professional dancers that hail from across the country, from New York's stages to California's showstoppers, and especially to the pop sensation and Broadway star who generously donated her time to perform for us… Paige McCall!" Jennifer waited as the crowd enthusiastically showed their appreciation. "Finally, to Nicki Long, a Broadway performer and our very own star, who now shares her time and talent with hopeful young girls who dream of a life on stage, such as the ones who've danced their way into our hearts tonight!"

A movement offstage caught Nicki's eyes. They widened a bit as she saw Julian coming up the stairs carrying a gigantic bouquet of large, perfectly formed red, yellow, pink and purple roses. Her heart skipped a beat. He'd been there. He'd seen the dance!

"For the show's choreographer and star," Jennifer gushed as Julian handed her the flowers.

The show's star, of course. Nicki's smile didn't falter as she accepted the bouquet.

"Because of tonight's success, we are well on our way to breaking ground for the Performing Arts of Paradise Center in Paradise Cove, opening by the summer of next year." Jennifer turned to Nicki. "Please, a few words to our patrons. She's not big on public speaking," Jennifer explained as she handed over the microphone.

"No, I'm not," Nicki agreed, clearing her throat to speak more loudly. "However, doing so is much easier tonight after receiving such amazing and genuine appreciation for this show. I've danced on Broadway. But nothing tops the way you've all made me feel tonight." She included Jennifer and Julian in her gaze around the auditorium. "Thank you."

And then it hit her. Of course. Why not? The idea was

crazy. Unorthodox. Scary. But what did she have to lose? All these thoughts whirled in her head in a matter of seconds.

Her eyes became misty as she eyed first him and then the crowd. Crazy how a broken ankle had prematurely ended a dream and at the same time catapulted her into a fantasy beyond any she could have imagined. For that she thanked everyone, even Vince. She thanked them, and she meant it. Julian, too. Even if he never asked her to be his wife again, she'd be his woman forever. But he hadn't asked her. And he probably wouldn't. So what if…

"Ladies and gentlemen, there's one more thing. I'm sorry, I won't be long, but there is one thing that tops even tonight's performance and your enthusiastic support." She turned to face Julian. "It is the love I feel for this man, Dr. Julian Drake."

Murmurs rippled through the crowd, followed by applause. She turned back to the crowd.

"A few years ago, in a wonderful moment in Times Square, he asked me to marry him. And I did something really stupid. I said no."

Gasps. Murmurs.

"I wasn't ready. I'm a dancer. A showgirl. My life is the stage. That's what I thought. But tonight, this is what I know."

She turned back to Julian as a single tear escaped and slid down her cheek. "My life on the stage isn't the same without you in it. I wish I'd said yes that night. Having hurt you the way I did, you'd be crazy to ask me again. So I'll ask you."

The audience became completely still. One could hear a feather fall.

"This wasn't preplanned, so I don't have a ring. What I do have is my love. My heart. And this question. Julian—" Nicki cried openly now. "Will you marry me?"

The entire audience held its breath.

She held up the mike. Julian slowly pulled it from her grasp, their eyes locked seemingly for centuries, though only mere seconds passed. He shifted, lifted the mike up to his mouth.

"No, Nicki. I can't do that."

Chapter 30

Julian heard the crowd noise gain in intensity, watched tiny beads of sweat mix with the tears running freely down Nicki's face and over the tendrils that clung to her skin, saw her lips quiver as she struggled for control. He'd never seen her look more radiant or beautiful. Her smile wide and eyes bright, even tinged with the slightest hint of regret he'd glimpsed when handing her the flowers. He felt that she loved him deeply, even after she'd said no to marrying him that time he proposed. Knew that in her mind Paradise Cove was temporary. A mere speed bump on her road back to a career on Broadway. The place she'd dreamed of dancing since seeing her first live show there, *The Lion King*, at ten years old.

He knew all of this, and he knew something else. For a Drake the word *no* was a mere speed bump, too, when it came to something they wanted. Yes, he'd just told Nicki no. But he wasn't finished talking. He held up his hand. The audience fell silent, as though he was their conductor.

"You know I love you, Nicki. Feels like I always have, like, since the beginning of time. When I said no just now, it was because of being the type of man I am—maybe it's that Drake thing. I know you're independent. That it's the twenty-first century and traditions have changed. But I couldn't let you play my position. Sweetheart…"

He reached into his pocket, pulled out an aqua-blue box.

"You're the very beat of my heart, the lulu of my life. And while you may have many others in your long and illustrious dance career, I want to be your one and only permanent dance partner."

Several women in the audience joined Nicki in wiping away tears.

"I asked you once. If necessary, I'd ask a thousand times. But I hope that tonight, I'll get the right answer."

He got down on one knee. The audience could barely contain themselves, a symphony of whistles, claps, murmurs and shushes providing the background music to Julian's declaration.

He raised his voice above the din. "Nicki Long—"

"Yes!"

"Will you do me the honor—"

"Yes!" Nicki screamed again, now laughing and crying at the same time.

Julian smiled broadly. "Let me finish, love. Will you make me the happiest man in the room by agreeing to marry me and to becoming my Mrs. Drake?"

"Yes!" Nicki shouted for a third time.

Jennifer whooped. The dancers jumped. Nicki grabbed the microphone, shouted louder.

"Yes, Dr. Julian Drake. I'll marry you!"

There was no mistaking her words this time. She'd shouted them through tears before throwing her arms around his neck and planting a whopper of a kiss smackdab on his lips. Jennifer cried, too, and dabbed her cheeks with the back of her hand. Julian pulled out a handkerchief and wiped Nicki's tears before handing it to Jennifer.

The crowd applauding, the dancers cheering, he took Nicki into his arms.

"I almost passed out when you said no," she whispered.

"I shouldn't have scared you." He wrapped her arms around his neck. "I just wanted to secure you."

She kissed him again. He parted his lips. Her tongue scorched his mouth. His tongue darted out in search of hers, created an oral tango worthy of any stage. He felt himself harden—Nicki's nipples, too. Nicki giggled, embarrassed. He knew that she felt him. Knew they needed to maintain the position until both calmed down. He handed his mother the mike.

"Now that's a finale," Jennifer exclaimed. "Thanks again, everyone. Good night!"

She walked off the stage. The dancers, too. The audience slowly filed out of the auditorium. Nicki and Julian remained where they were, two hearts beating as one for several minutes. They basked in the moment, in no hurry to leave. It had taken almost six years and two tries to get this commitment. For Julian, this lifetime dance of decadent desire had been more than worth the wait.

Backstage was a crush. Nicki smiled until her face felt frozen. Posed, shook hands and gave hugs across the room. Finally she made her way to the dressing room, where in the privacy of the room filled with flowers she spent ten glorious minutes with Julian.

"Baby, I need to shower and dress real quick. We've still got the private party, remember?"

Julian tightened his hold, pulled her even closer. "I'm enjoying the private party we're having right now."

Fifteen minutes later, they left the building through a side door. Nicki shivered against the chilly night air and wrapped her coat even tighter around her.

Julian noticed and placed his arm around her. "You want to wait inside while I go get the car?"

"How far away is it?"

"Just down the street. But your head isn't covered, and I don't want you to get sick."

"I grew up in cold weather, babe. Let's just hurry. I'll be fine."

She threaded her arm through his as they rounded the building and, once on the sidewalk, picked up the pace.

"Nicki!"

She stopped abruptly at the sound of her name. She shivered again, this time not from the cold. But from recognizing the voice of who'd called out to her. A quick glance around confirmed the fear. Vince.

"Let's keep walking." She urged Julian forward.

Vince called out again. "Nicki, wait."

He stopped. "Babe, who is that?" She looked at him, aware as the answer dawned in his eyes. "Wait here."

He turned and began walking swiftly toward Vince, his hands balled into fists.

"Julian!"

Vince held up his hands, began a fast retreat. "Hey, man. I don't want any trouble. Just need to apologize to Nicki, that's all."

Julian stopped with a couple of feet between them. Nicki reached his side and grabbed his coat sleeve. Tension emanated from Julian's body. Coiled, controlled, ready to pounce.

She glared at Vince as he began to speak.

"I'm sorry, Nicki. About everything. Hopefully one day you'll be able to forgive me. I had a problem back then that had me out of control. It's no excuse, but I was addicted. To gambling. A habit worse than drugs. One I couldn't control. Ironically, you played a part in my healing. Ran into this girl on my way out of town, out of Paradise Cove. I'd hit bottom. A weak moment. Poured out my heart. She suggested a program called Gamblers Anonymous. I looked it up and found one here. So instead of going back to New York, I stayed out West. Got well. Now I hear she's in trouble. Anyway, that's a whole other story."

"You ran into Natalie?" Julian asked.

"I ran into Ashley, who introduced me to Nat. Do you know her? Never mind. I forgot. Small town."

Nicki shivered again.

Julian reached for her hand. "Let's go, babe."

She looked at Vince. "I forgive you, okay? And I'm glad you got help."

"Thank you." And to Julian. "I'm sorry, man."

Julian nodded. They turned and hurried to the car, Nicki easily matching Julian's long strides. She never looked back. There was no need. The only man she wanted was walking beside her.

* * * * *

*If you enjoyed this sexy story, pick up
these other titles in Zuri Day's*
THE DRAKES OF CALIFORNIA *series:*

*CRYSTAL CARESS
SILKEN EMBRACE
SAPPHIRE ATTRACTION
LAVISH LOVING*

Available now from Harlequin Kimani Romance!

COMING NEXT MONTH
Available November 21, 2017

#549 SEDUCED BY THE TYCOON AT CHRISTMAS
The Morretti Millionaires • by Pamela Yaye

Italy's most powerful businessman, Romeo Morretti, spends his days brokering multimillion-dollar deals, but an encounter with Zoe Smith sends his life in a new direction. When secrets threaten their passionate bond, Romeo must fight to clear his name before they can share a future under the mistletoe.

#550 A LOVE LIKE THIS
Sapphire Shores • by Kianna Alexander

All action star Devon Granger wants for Christmas is a peaceful escape to his hometown. How is he to rest with Hadley Monroe tending to his every need? And when the media descends on the beachfront community, their dreams of ringing in the New Year together could be out of their grasp…

#551 AN UNEXPECTED HOLIDAY GIFT
The Kingsleys of Texas • by Martha Kennerson

When a scuffle leads to community service, basketball star Keylan "KJ" Kingsley opts to devote his hours to his family's foundation. Soon he plunges into a relationship with charity executive Mia Ramirez. When KJ returns to the court, will his celebrity status risk the family that could be theirs by Christmas?

#552 DESIRE IN A KISS
The Chandler Legacy • by Nicki Night

On impulse, heir to a food empire Christian Chandler creates a fake dating profile and quickly connects with petite powerhouse Serenity Williams. She's smart, down-to-earth and ignites his fantasies from their first encounter. But how can he admit the truth to a woman for whom honesty is everything?

Get 2 Free Books,
Plus 2 Free Gifts—
just for trying the Reader Service!

 KIMANI™ ROMANCE